LOVE IS KIND

A CHRISTIAN ROMANCE

LOVE IS
BOOK 2

FAITH ARCENEAUX

✝

 Created with Vellum

NEWSLETTER

I pray this story will inspire you, and at the least entertain you.

If you love it, and want to be the first to hear about the next release, join my newsletter.

Join Here: https://bit.ly/faith2love

ONE

Leah

Vice President of Creative would sound amazing. Especially with my name attached to the front of it. If things went my way, they'd be updating the company website with my new title.

Before going to the office though, I stopped at Cup of Sunshine on the corner to grab my team some muffins. They deserved more than muffins for how they helped me succeed. Until my raise took effect, that was all I could afford to splurge. Between paying off my student loan debt and repaying my parents, I was running on a strict budget. So, I hoped muffins would do.

With an upturned face, I ordered the dozen muffins and thanked the woman as she handed them to me. Before walking out I said, "I hope you have an amazing day," over my shoulder.

I walked past Sara, the receptionist, with my shoulders straight, as I sang, "Good morning," to her. Her mumbled reply made me double back and ask, "Everything okay?"

She released a small smile as she sighed. "Another day in the office."

Another day in the office, for her. For me, it was the day I was getting promoted. *God willing.*

I continued into the kitchen to drop off the muffins. "Oh, for us?" Dan peered over my shoulder and had his fingers dangling before I could even respond. "Expecting good news today?" he asked.

"I'm praying," I told him as I moved out of his way so he would have unobstructed access to the muffins. With our performance reviews, I was waiting for the news I'd been waiting years to hear.

"Say a prayer for me too." He winked as he bit into one of the muffins.

I made it to my desk and opened the project file for the Stanley Group. The design elements I was working on would keep me occupied until it was time for me to meet with my boss, Margot.

The colors for the ad image were popping, but I couldn't get the text to convey the right message. Staring at the few lines I was adjusting had my eyes crossing. So much that that the notification on my screen startled me. I jumped and shook my head before dismissing it. I knew another would pop up a few minutes before I needed to walk into Margot's office.

The time on my laptop was earlier than it should have been. I searched my calendar for another meeting. There was one starting in ten minutes. I scrunched up my face and looked around as I opened the email to see who was invited. *The entire creative team.* Sitting in the conference room with my team was the last thing I needed to do. I assumed it was a meeting to discuss team performance. *Although we had a similar meeting last week.*

I chewed the side of my lip as I stood from my desk, ready to walk to the conference room. Kerry walked up beside me and asked, "Know what this is about?"

I shook my head. "No. You?"

She held up the palms of her hands and said, "Staffing announcements?" Her elbow nudged my side. "Ready for that, Ms. VP?"

I felt my cheeks warming as we made our way into the conference room. "Still haven't had my review yet, but I'm hoping that's the outcome."

Kerry was new to the team but brought a lot of knowledge from her prior agency. One of our competitors, Brown Brothers. "I mean, who else could they pick? You're a beast on these projects," she boasted as we sat beside each other.

I looked across the table at everyone else—any one of them could be a strong candidate. "There are a few people." My eyebrows bunched together as I looked back to Kerry. Before I could elaborate though, Margot rushed into the room.

She paced in front of the projector, paused with her hand on her hip, then looked around to each of us. Her eyes were glossy, and her black hair wasn't tucked into a ponytail like usual. The last time she looked anything like that, her puppy was sick and close to dying. Kerry leaned in closer to me and whispered, "What is going on?"

I hunched my shoulders, but my eyes were stuck on

Margot waiting for her to speak. The room was silent, except for the air conditioner that was blowing overhead.

"Bryer Marketing Agency..." Margot paused, taking another deep breath before wiping a hand across her face. "It has been acquired and our entire team is being released." Her eyes blinked shut, or mine did. Everything she said after that felt like it was traveling through earmuffs.

"How did we get acquired? I didn't even know that the agency was up for sale. Last week, our team was being heralded for our great work. What is going on? Why our team?" The questions were coming from my mouth like rapid fire, and others joined me with questions of their own.

Margot raised her hands to her head and swiped back the stray hairs, then her hands rested there. "This wasn't expected. As far as I know, nobody had advanced knowledge. I mean, if I would have known," she shook her head, "I wouldn't have stayed up preparing performance reviews last night." Her eyes glanced my way. "But," she blew out a puff of air, "that isn't the worst of it. Today is our last day and we need to clean out our desks."

Dan stood from his side of the table and flipped his notepad over. "You're kidding me. You can't be serious right now." He laughed nervously. "Margot, this is a joke, right? Some deranged role play for a new client or something?" He looked around the room like someone was going to pop out of a corner. As crazy as it sounded, I prayed that it was all a joke. Some type of skit.

Then Margot announced, "I wish that was the case. These folders contain your severance packages. Read them carefully." As she passed them around, tears fell from her eyes. "If you decide to accept the terms, you'll need to return the signed copy to HR before you leave."

The folder laid open in front of me. When I pulled the stapled papers from the pocket, my eyes scanned the words before reading *one month's pay.*

"What are we supposed to do with this?" Kerry's voice bounced off the walls as everyone sat reading through their own papers. "I left Brown to come here, and now this?" Her gripes echoed by those around us.

My eyes closed as I thought about what would happen if the other agencies weren't hiring. Or if I couldn't find something before the month was over. The thought of updating my resume, after not touching it much in ten years, was daunting.

One month's salary wouldn't last. It wouldn't take long for my savings to dwindle if I needed to use what little I had there. I tapped my leg and re-opened my eyes, looking at the folder again. It wasn't like anything had changed. The terms were still the same. I was fired from the job I poured into for years.

God, I know you work everything for my good. I heard that recited often. Listened to sermons where they preached it. And for years I believed it, but that day, I couldn't understand how He'd work it out for my good. I couldn't understand how in an instant my dreams felt crushed. How the result would be anything that resembled *good.*

I closed the folder, ready to get out of the conference room. There was nothing left I could do there. But as I stood, I saw Margot sitting alone, tears streaming down her face, and I walked over to her. With a hand on her shoulder, I managed to tease, "This is not how I thought our conversation would go today."

The sorrow in her eyes and her downturned lips felt too heavy. Not as heavy as her body as it collapsed into mine though. Her arms wrapped tight around me, and the two of us embraced for who knows how long.

"Leah, I'm sorry. It's not how I expected it would go either. I was completely blindsided." She released me. With a lowered voice, she said, "If I would have known, we all could have found something else before now." She jerked her head toward Kerry. "Imagine, I wouldn't have even hired her. She would have been better off at Brown."

Kerry's face looked as miserable as Margot's, and I could only imagine mine looked the same.

"Maybe so." From the stories Kerry shared about Brown, it had its pitfalls. A little more than the workplace drama we experienced at Bryer.

The conference room was clearing, and Margot said, "I'm going to clean my desk out." Her shoulders slumped. "I don't know if hurts to hear this now, but if all this didn't happen, you would have gotten that promotion."

It wasn't like the sting of a paper cut, it felt more like a kick to the gut. I reached for my shirt and clutched it between my fingers to ease the aching sensation. "It hurts more than you know." Leaving the conference room, it felt worse. If that was even possible.

On my desk sat a large box that wasn't there before the meeting. Beside it, instructions to return my devices. Nowhere between was an apology. Not a stitch of emotion that seemed regretful to inform us of the decision. I grabbed a pen from the drawer, scribbled my name across the severance letter, and shut the folder.

In less time than it would have taken me to draft an email,

I had my industry books, notebooks, pens, and pictures piled high in the single box. I balanced it on my waist and wandered down the hall into HR to drop off the signed paper. It pained me to even look into Benny's eyes. He was one of the people who interviewed me for the job at Bryer. The person who extended my offer of employment with a cheerful voice.

"We couldn't have received a heads up?"

His lips pulled tight before he replied, "Leah, I'm sorry."

I tried to hold my head up high as I walked from his office, but it felt dreadful.

When I started at Bryer, I was fresh out of grad school and ready to put my degree to work. Or as my parents said, "Get out of our pockets." They did all they could to help me during school. But the little they could spare was only enough to buy a book or two each semester. The first paycheck I received from Bryer, I took them out to dinner and promised I'd repay them for every dollar they sent my way. Since then, I was able to do that and a little more.

The box I was carrying was heavy, but the weight on my shoulders was starting to bare down on me. A brief look at the rows of desks, the people still seated. One last memory of the place I walked into with excitement five days a week, or more, and my eyes glossed over.

The somber look on Sara's face as I passed was much different than earlier that morning. She said, "Leah, I wish you the best."

"Thanks, Sara," I said as I stood in front of the elevator doors.

When they opened, two people I'd never seen before stepped off. As I stepped past them, I said, "Have a good day," like I was leaving for the night and would return in the morning.

The elevator doors were closing as the man paused. His eyebrows gathered, and his deep brown eyes narrowed. Nothing fell from his mouth in response though. His chiseled jawline, edged fade, chocolate complexion, and tailored suit was the last image I had of the Bryer Agency.

TWO

Deshaun

When I heard, "The Bryer Marketing Agency is in trouble," I snapped into action. After a couple of weeks of negotiation, Mr. Bryer himself was out, and I was in. My portfolio expanding to numbers that impressed me.

I couldn't say I was as thrilled to be back home though. As I passed a woman walking into the office building, I frowned. All smiles, and a fresh, "Good afternoon," reminded me how different Greensboro was from New York City. I would miss the ability to navigate the streets without talking to a single soul.

"Mr. Green," Coco started as she trailed behind me. "You aren't even going to respond to her?"

"For what?" I smirked as I walked through the opened door.

"Or say thank you to the man who held your door?"

"Can you repeat the list of tasks I've given you so far," I asked as we stood in front of the elevator. "I've already wasted enough time sitting in the broker's office, I don't have time to meander."

Coco was scrolling through her tablet when the doors of the elevator opened. "Looks like there are some disgruntled employees."

"Ex," I noted.

She tilted her head to the side.

"Disgruntled *ex-employees*." The elevator stopped a few floors before our destination, but I didn't budge when the people tried to enter. *They could step around.* "I'm not worried about the feelings of *ex-employees*."

Coco cleared her throat, and I looked over my shoulder at the woman who squeezed onto the elevator. Her eyes were wide and watching. I didn't care, but Coco remained silent for the rest of the ride.

We made it to the third floor, and when the elevator doors opened again a woman was standing in front of them with a box. I moved past her as she entered the elevator then heard her say, "Have a great day," as the doors closed.

"Southern Hospitality will be the end of me," I told Coco, "Make that list number," I waved my hand toward her, "whatever. Make sure the employees know I don't need pleasantries. When they speak to me, tell them I don't have time for small talk."

"Great," she mumbled. "Task number four..." With her eyes narrowed, she continued with the remaining six as we made our way to my new office. "And eleven," she concluded, "don't be nice to the boss."

Coco had been my assistant for years. Although I never

told her, she had the ability to deal with my *terse* personality better than anyone in my life. Being from New York voided her of the Southern Hospitality I despised. I didn't have to issue her a warning to mind my time. But over the years, her sarcasm took over.

So, I reminded her, "Add 'sarcasm is never necessary' to that reminder to the employees."

She sucked her teeth and tapped into her tablet before telling me, "Noted. Anything else, Mr. Green?" Her cocked eyebrow let me know she was over me for the day, and that was fine because I didn't need much else from her.

"Yes." I examined the space that was once occupied by Mr. Bryer and said, "Send a bottle of champagne to Jacob."

"At the Brown Agency?" she asked with a high-pitched voice.

"None other," I noted as I rubbed my hand along the wooden desk.

"But you are new to town, shouldn't he be sending you a bottle of champagne?"

I hunched my shoulders and leaned against the desk. "Be sure to add a note that reads..." I cleared my throat. "May the best man win."

Jacob Brown was the CEO and co-owner of the Brown Brothers Agency, one of Bryer's biggest competitors. One of few Black-owned marketing agencies in the city. Another agency with a multi-million-dollar portfolio. He could have snapped up Bryer, if only I left it on the table long enough.

"Okay," Coco responded, "I can do that."

Rubbing my hands together, I walked to the window overlooking the nearby park. "Good, can't wait to hear his response."

Not only was Jacob one of my steepest competitors, but he also happened to be a childhood friend. Outside of our companies, the two of us had a crazy bond. He was one of the only people outside of my family I trusted. Learning how I stole Bryer from under his nose would upset him. Before now, our business never stepped on each other's toes. We could maintain our friendship without crossing boundaries.

It was something I considered before moving home. But when I learned about the breadth of Bryer's clients and the earning potential, I didn't care if I crossed an imaginary line or not.

Coco's loud sigh reminded me she was still standing in the office with me. "Now, is that all?"

"It is." I nodded without turning to face her.

"Great," with an extra sweet tone, she said, "have a *great weekend.*"

Her weekend was starting, but mine would have a delay, if it'd happen at all. Buying Bryer was a risk. Although they had a deep client roster, Mr. Bryer must have been swindling cash because the accounts were in the red. With my eyes on the books, I'd have to strategize, determine how I'd turn things around. And if I managed it as I did my other agencies, I'd have it turned around within months. *Guaranteed.*

Before I could fire up my laptop to review files, there was a light tap at the door. In walked Benny, the head of Bryer HR. He stood at the door as he waited for me to signal he could enter. I appreciated that much and said, "C'mon in." As he stood a few feet in front of me, I asked, "Did you need something?"

"It's the severance package." He cleared his throat. "Sir, not everyone accepted the terms." He swiped a finger beneath his collar then was bolder with his approach as he stated, "And I can't blame them. The terms are far from acceptable."

"Last I checked, I was the CEO and made all the determining decisions." I stood from behind the desk and squared my shoulders. "I'm not concerned with those who didn't accept the terms. Those who didn't will save us a month's worth of salary."

Benny looked annoyed, but he'd learn I couldn't care less whether he was or not.

When he didn't budge, I tilted my head to the side and asked, "Was there something else?"

He shook his head and mumbled, "I guess that's it," before he turned to walk away. As he reached the door, he said, "I hope you have a great weekend."

I snatched my phone from my desk, clicking Coco's number. As soon as she answered, I blurted, "That employee notice. Task eleven, and twelve, or whatever." I let her catch up with what I was saying. "That needs to go out today. It can't wait until Monday."

She laughed until she didn't hear mine on the other end. "You're serious?"

"Get it done," I yelled before hanging up.

THREE

Leah

I thought the morning after getting fired would be the worst. I was wrong, and the pastel pink walls of my childhood bedroom were a good reminder. The other was the way my leg fell over the side of the daybed—dangling to the point I could no longer feel my toes.

The worst.

Sunshine had barely graced the blinds, but I needed to get up out of my bed. The act of trying to sleep was becoming more challenging. It wasn't worth the few more minutes I would have gained.

I stretched my arms over head and said, "Thank you, God, for another day." My prayers had started to become less and less elaborate over the weeks since losing my job. I understood the call to pray without ceasing, but it felt like a reminder of what wasn't answered. Job posting after job posting, I submitted my resume. Still not a single interview got scheduled.

With my toiletries in hand, I made my way to the shared bathroom in the hallway. I knocked lightly to make sure nobody was on the other side. It was all clear, so I entered. The stream of water was only on for a few seconds before I climbed inside the shower. I rubbed soap over my body, then rinsed and wrapped myself in my robe to head back to my room.

Long showers and privacy were a luxury of the past. One I had to give up when my bank account started nearing zero. There was one silver lining in everything that happened—my parents were in the city, and I was able to move back home. Although it was the last place I expected to be in my thirties.

Because I didn't have a job, and nothing to occupy my time, I spent most of my day at the community center volunteering. So, I dressed in a pair of leggings and an oversized shirt. I walked to the kitchen for breakfast. *Another silver lining, time to enjoy breakfast in the morning.*

"Headed to the community center?" my dad asked with a smug look on his face.

"Good morning, Daddy," I said, wrapping my arms around his neck to hug him. "Yes, I'm headed to the community center."

He grumbled, "You should ask your brother if he could get you a paying job there."

It was one of his constant reminders, for me to find a *paying* job, like it wasn't the highest item on my priority list. I informed him, "I applied to a few more places yesterday, but still nothing."

My mom walked into the kitchen beaming from ear to ear as she sang, "Good morning, Leah." Unlike my dad, she appreciated me being home. Maybe a little too much. At night we'd sit on the couch and binge watch shows together. It was the most time we spent together in years.

"Good morning, Mama." I kissed her cheek.

She plucked my shirt and asked, "Headed to the center again today?"

As I roamed the refrigerator for something to eat, I told her, "I am. If I can't help myself, at least I can help someone else."

"Your brother called the other day and mentioned how useful it's been." My mom was leaning over the coffee machine.

"Told her to ask him for a paying position." Dad moved from the table and placed his plate in the sink. "I mean, if she's been so helpful it should be easy to convince them to hire her."

My shoulders slumped because the only jobs I applied to were for marketing positions. I'd seen others, some I did not have the skillset for, others that wouldn't pay enough for me to afford my bills. "Daddy, I'm sure something will come up." *If only I could be as confident.*

"Leah," he stood beside me, "baby girl, if there was anything more we could do, we would. But I don't know if we'll be able to help much once your money runs out. You have to find something in the meantime. Something that'll deposit a little change in your account."

My eyes glossed over, and it felt like the room had swallowed me whole. I didn't receive a graduate degree for a *little change*. But I got it, my parents could no more help me now than they could back when I was in school. I didn't want to be an undue burden, not when they should have been enjoying life. "I'll find something," I promised. "I'll see you two later this evening." I left the kitchen before the tears could fall down my face.

On my way to the center, I had a serious conversation with God. I couldn't call it a prayer, because it was time for me to *hear* what He had to say.

"God." I blew a long stream of air from my mouth. "We've always been good. Before now, life was steady. Hardly encountered any bumps. And I'm not sure I prepared for this crater in the middle of the road. Still, I recognize that your will is better than my own." I tapped my foot on the brake as the light turned red. "God, guide me. Lead me. I'll do what it is you need me to do."

The light was still red, a line of people crossing at the crosswalk. *Bryer Marketing Agency.* I didn't even realize I was in front of the building. The sight of the words still made my stomach churn. "God, get me past this," I pleaded.

Then, like a light was illuminating it, I saw a "Now Hiring" sign on the coffee shop next door.

As the light turned green, I looked up to the sky and whispered, "You sure, God?" with my eyebrows stitched together. For the first time in a couple of months, I felt an odd peace wash over me.

Still, I ignored it. I parked in front of the community center. Walking inside, I thought my brother could have a different solution. Like my dad suggested, they could hire me.

The volunteers inside were a different cast and crew during the daytime. But like the ones I worked with in the evening, they were pleasant. One woman, Marcy, was in the dining room when I walked by. She shouted, "Hey, Leah, happy to see you here again," with a wave of her hand.

Stepping inside the door, I asked her, "How can I help

today?" Needs varied from day to day, but I wasn't opposed to helping in any way possible. The people the community center served were in need—of a meal, a place to lay their head, or clothes to wear.

"Mitch mentioned needing some help sorting the clothes delivered yesterday." She continued stacking chairs. "Or you know, they always need help in the kitchen."

I winked and said, "I'll go find, Mitch." I wasn't the best person in the kitchen. Although when Ms. Carol was volunteering, she had a way of taking my lack of skill and making a tasty side dish. Before I went to the storage room I stopped in Liam's office. "Hey, Liam," I said, tapping on his door to get his attention.

"Leah," he cringed, "I guess you being here means you haven't found a job yet, huh?" Then he raised his hands. "But don't get me wrong, the director appreciates you volunteering more."

Standing across from his desk, I said, "I'm glad you weren't about to ride me like Dad. He let me know I need to find something ASAP." I decided that was the perfect segue into what he suggested. "Thinks there could be a paid position here." I laughed nervously.

"Here?" he repeated with his head jerking backward. "I wish there was something available." He slouched in his chair. "With a steady flow of volunteers, they may never think there's a need to hire more staff. We could use more help, from people who we pay to be consistent. You know?"

"Makes sense. But, I'm not going to stress over it." Remembering the sign at the coffee shop, I said, "Cup of Sunshine is hiring."

Liam's eyes widened. "The coffee shop next to your old

building?" I nodded. "That would be a little awkward, don't you think?"

I hadn't put much thought into it. "Desperate times call for desperate measures." I wiped the back of my neck. "Like Daddy said, at this point I need to be putting money *in* my account."

He pointed. "That part." His nose crinkled as he said, "But I'm pretty sure those coins won't compare to what you were making at Bryer."

I shook my head. "It won't." Then I told him, "Something is better than nothing, I guess." As he started to offer his help, I said, "Thanks, bro, really. But I can't ask for your help any easier than Mom and Dad. It's not like you are rolling in the dough either."

He laughed. "Out here living a life of charity and such."

"Speaking of which, I should let you get back to it. I'm helping Mitch sort through the clothes." Standing next to his door, I told him, "If you want to help, pray I can qualify as a barista."

He steepled his hands together. "I got you."

FOUR

Deshaun

"Coco," I screamed from my office. When she didn't appear, I shouted again, "Coco." With a desk right outside my door, her response should have been immediate.

Finally, when she walked into the office with little urgency, she said, "Yes, Mr. Green?" Her voice was brusque, but I ignored that as I pointed to my screen.

"Have you seen these numbers?" I stood from my desk and started pacing. "We've been operating for three months now. We are no closer to turning things around than we were when we acquired Bryer."

Coco wasn't anyone who could help me fix things. She couldn't quality check the creative or run lead in the sales department. She could call a staff meeting with all the heads of the department though. Because she didn't suggest it, I told her, "All the heads, ASAP."

"Got it," she said, walking from my office. She poked her head in a few minutes later and said, "They'll meet you in the conference room now. Would you like me to capture notes?"

I snatched my laptop from my desk and told her, "Unless you have something better to do." I walked into the conference room and was glad that everyone was already seated around the table.

"Which one of you can tell me why we are bleeding clients?" I looked around the table at faces that were new to me, and ones I'd worked with for years. "What is going on?" I was barking questions until a brave soul decided to respond.

Claire from the sales team spoke up, telling me, "The number of proposals we have lost is unprecedented. And the feedback from existing clients is that they want the old team."

"The old team?" I repeated. "That's nonsense. Our team is skilled and would likely run circles around the old team." My eyes were on the creative director, Nancy, from the New York office. "This is on your team. What are you doing to correct it?"

"Greensboro isn't like New York." She sat up in her seat and continued, "The clients here are not interested in our designs and methods."

I scratched my fingers across my head, then adjusted my tie. The room grew silent. Everyone was watching me, waiting for me to give a directive. In many of our previous meetings, I gave them their marching orders and expected they'd execute. From what I was seeing in the revenue reports, that couldn't have been what they were doing.

Nate cowered in a corner until I asked, "And this is what you are seeing in the customer feedback?" He nodded.

"We need to retain who we have if we can't gain new clients right now. Claire, offer a discount."

Nancy raised her hand like I was teaching an elementary school class. "What is it, Nancy?" I asked.

"Well, if I may, we need time to figure out what the other team's cutting edge was. Even if we offer them a discount and they aren't satisfied, they'll be looking to leave." That garnered a few grumbles around the table.

"Go through the notes, old client files, project deliveries. By the end of the day tomorrow, I want a report of your findings on my desk."

Claire fidgeted with her pen, but she didn't argue my directive.

"Nancy, who are most of the new clients signing with?" I looked to Coco to make sure she was capturing the response.

"Mostly, Brown Brothers. But it varies, the most recent one was to the Fusion Group."

I sucked my teeth. It wasn't what I wanted to hear, but if it had to be anybody other than me, at least it was Jacob. "Got it. I'll be awaiting the report tomorrow." I nodded toward Coco, and she stood to follow me out of the conference room. "There's a networking event tonight. Jacob will be there. I need you to come and be my eyes and ears on his team, and others who may be in attendance."

"But—"

"I'm leaving at seven. You can ride with me."

"Great, I'll be ready." Her mouth tightened and she clutched her tablet against her chest.

I walked into my office and closed the door behind me. I didn't emerge until a few minutes before it was time to leave.

The office had cleared out, but I could hear small chatter on the floor.

"Ready to leave?" Coco had her purse over her shoulder.

"Yes." I started toward the elevator. "I'm in the garage," I told her as I punched the button for the floor. "Once it's over I'll drop you back at the garage."

"Thanks, so kind of you," she mumbled under her breath without looking at me.

"Now." I ignored her commentary. "When we get to the lounge, I need you to start with his assistant, and see if you can gather any information from her. Then spread out, I need to find out what clients find appealing about their companies."

"At a networking event? You think I'll be able to get those details at a networking event?"

I nodded. "Yes, I do." I unlocked the car and climbed into the driver's seat. The car started before she climbed in on the passenger side.

"Since it's after hours, and technically, I'm not on the clock, I have the liberty to say this..." She paused as if I was going to grant her permission to proceed. When I didn't, she continued anyway, "You lack all decorum of a gentleman."

"Is there more?" I asked as I drove through the city. It wasn't like I didn't attend Jack & Jill growing up. I learned how to be a *gentleman.* My mother ensured my siblings and I attended all the etiquette training available to us. She made sure we *knew how to act in public.* I didn't need to share that with Coco though. As far as I was concerned, none of that applied at work.

Her narrow finger ended up in my peripheral as she boasted, "See, you don't even care." A sound of distress in her voice.

"There's a difference between me caring and something being relevant. You think the work hour stopped when you left the building. We are colleagues, and that courtesy never expires. If the idea came to mind because I didn't open your door, well, that's not something I do for colleagues." That was putting it nicely.

She scoffed and crossed her arms over her chest. "I hope this doesn't last long."

"We'll be traveling to New York in a week." I looked her way. "Being in the south is getting to you." She didn't find my comment the least bit funny.

I valeted the car and as we walked toward the door, I said, "Let me grab this for you before you forget what you are here to do." I concentrated on her firm face. "So, we are clear, you are here to gather information, and you are still working."

She saluted me and said, "Got it, Mr. Green," before disappearing.

While many gathered around the bar, I searched for Jacob among the crowd. I found him surrounded by varying women. *His typical MO.*

"Mr. Brown," I said as I approached him with my hand outstretched.

He laughed and asked, "Do you see my brother around here?" His eyes narrowed. "He's the only one pretentious enough to call *mister.*" He pulled me into a tight hug. In my ear, he whispered, "Not sure I appreciate seeing you during the week knowing you are now in my territory." He cleared his throat and backed away. "By the way, I hope you received that bottle of Korbel I sent."

I shook my head as I watched his mouth form into a menacing smirk. "I poured it into the toilet where it belongs." I looked around us and said, "How about you introduce me to your friends?"

"Ladies, gentlemen," he announced as his head swiveled, "this is the newest kid on the block, Mr. Green. He's taken over the Bryer Agency here in the city."

"Yes." I straightened my back. "And plan on bringing my breadth of experience from my global brand."

A man across from me questioned, "Oh, that was brave. Heard Bryer was doing pretty bad."

My jaw tensed, but I held my head straight as I said, "Was." I eyed Jacob. "Bryer will meet the standards of my other agencies soon enough."

The same man snickered. "Fusion welcomes the competition." He raised his glass in the air before saying, "May the competition all make us stronger."

"Stronger," Jacob's hand tapped my back, "exactly what we all need, right, Deshaun?" But his eyes went over my shoulder as his facial expression changed. "Wait, is that..."

"Who?" I turned over my shoulder and watched Coco striding our way. "Coco?" My eyes widened, but Jacob's were slanting.

He guzzled the rest of his drink before he stepped around me. "Coco, long time no see?" His hand outstretched to hers.

Her face turned from a scorn to a smile as he neared her ear. I hoped however close the two got, she could use it to Bryer's advantage.

FIVE

Leah

Instead of a silk blouse and accompanying slacks, I was in a pair of black jeans, a black t-shirt, and a pair of black sneakers. On top of that, I had on an apron.

As I walked past Bryer, I plucked at my apron and said, "At least I'm working." I opened the door to Cup of Sunshine. A long line greeted me.

Behind the counter, Jace was taking orders. I made my way toward her. Shouting, "I'll be right out," as I ran to the back to clock-in

I tapped Jace's shoulder and told her, "I got the next one," when I returned. Jace hated interacting with customers.

The line was still extended toward the front. "How can I help you?" I recited the same words more than I could remember. The muscles in my cheeks ached from smiling for each customer.

"The rush is over," Jace announced as she flung a towel on the counter. "A little break before people need their second cup." She pulled her phone from her pocket. "Maybe people will skip it today," she grumbled. As she scrolled her phone I wiped counters then refilled straws and sugar.

The front door opened, and I heard, "Leah," in a sing song voice.

"Janine?" I asked as I watched her cross the café. "What are you doing here?" I narrowed my eyes.

She got close enough to wrap me in her arms before she replied, "I was on this side of town for a meeting and decided to visit." She cringed. "I hope it's okay."

"Of course." I wrapped my arms around her neck. "And you're in luck, we aren't busy." I led her to the back of the restaurant and pointed to a chair. "If you have a few minutes, let's sit."

Janine sat across from me. "Will you be at the brunch tomorrow?"

I frowned, then reminded her, "Girl, the way my bank account is set up."

She hissed. "Right." Then her face crinkled up. "I know you don't want any help, but I can treat. It's been a while since you've been out with us. We miss you."

"I miss you all too." I'd skipped every brunch since I was fired. Outside of Janine, I had hardly seen my other friends. But anything involving outside became even more expensive when my funds dried up.

"Let me treat. That's what friends are for." Janine looked around the coffee shop and said, "I'm pretty sure, you'll be able to repay me soon." An enormous smile spread across her face.

I nodded my head and looked to the door where a

customer was entering. "I'm remaining hopeful," I told her. "God didn't get me through four years of college and a master's program to stick me in a coffee shop where I'm not using any of it." Jace was behind the counter, still scrolling on her phone. "It has humbled me though."

She huffed. "What if God put me in your life to help so that you can still enjoy brunch with your girls?"

I laughed. "I guess that could be possible." I snickered. "How about I go with you to brunch if you come with me to church?" I wriggled my shoulders.

Janine looked to her side before looking back at me with a twitch in her eye. "Church?" She grasped at her neck. "This weekend? On Sunday?" Her nose crinkled, and I knew she was thinking of an excuse she could give me. Despite all the excuses she could imagine, I wouldn't stop inviting her. "I have some errands I'll need to run." She stood from the seat. "But hey, the offer for brunch still stands. I'll even pick you up, so you don't have to use your gas."

I stood along with her. "Okay."

She linked her arm through mine. "Great, I'll pick you up tomorrow at ten."

"See you tomorrow at ten." I pulled my arm from hers and waved as she walked out the door.

The afternoon rush wouldn't hit us for a while, so I used the time to be like Jace and scroll on my phone. But where she was laughing at videos she watched, I was searching for jobs. Anything that could pay me more than what I was earning at Cup of Sunshine. There were administrative positions, teaching assistants at the college, and a few data analyst roles. Nothing that could use my experience. But as I heard the brew of the coffee machine, I thought, *Barista wasn't on my list of expertise either.*

I starred a few of the roles before the door swung open and let in the flood of afternoon customers. One after the other, I served up their orders. Each with a smile, and some with short conversations.

"Leah." A smiling Sara approached the counter. "I swear you are the highlight of my day. I miss seeing you in the office."

I laughed. "Sara, you smile more in here than I ever saw you smile in the office. How's everything today?" I grabbed a cup to make her order. After her first few visits I remembered it and made it from memory each time after.

Sara's smile disappeared. "It's not getting any better." In the times she visited she shared how the changes at Bryer were impacting the morale. How the new CEO was hard to work with. Even as the receptionist, she said he would criticize her warm welcomes to him. "Thinking I'll look for something else soon." Her head was on a swivel when she said that. "Better be careful in case there are listening ears," she said as I handed her the cup of coffee.

Her eyes were wide as she handed me her credit card. "Crap."

"Everything okay?" I asked, holding her card in the air.

"Oh, yes, go ahead." But her head jerked toward the back of the line. "That's him."

I craned my neck to see who she was referencing.

"Mr. Green."

My eyes narrowed. "Mr. Green?"

The customer behind her stepped to the counter, edging Sara out of the way. "I'll have a large coffee with one pump of vanilla, a pump of hazelnut, and a splash of oat milk."

I printed the order for Jace to start on, and after telling the customer, "It'll be right up," I searched the back of the line for *Mr. Green*. But Sara was long gone and couldn't confirm who he was, and why it mattered. The man at the end of the line did look familiar though.

"Let me get..." The woman standing in front of me blurted her order, then handed over her card without a greeting or a smile.

"It'll be right up," I said, ensuring my smile was a little wider.

The line continued, and after each customer I glanced at the man who was getting closer. Still, I couldn't place him. He wasn't a regular. I remembered most of them, and their orders.

Once I completed the order of the woman in front of him, I anticipated his approach. His voice could trigger my memory.

"Good afternoon." A wide smile spread across my face before I offered, "How can I help you?"

His eyes were above my head when he grumbled, "I don't even remember my order."

I watched as his face formed a scowl. "I can suggest our specialty."

"No," he said with a firm shake of his head. "I don't want the specialty. I want my order." He rubbed a hand across his well-manicured beard. Even with a scowl on his face, he was an attractive man. As he stared at the sign above my head, I stared at him. I admired his slanted eyes, his dark skin, and the muscles formed under his shirt.

"Sir," a woman shouted from behind him, "I need to get back to work. Could you hurry?"

"Espresso, cappuccino." I was listing off standard coffee

orders hoping his memory would be better than mine was being and he'd remember. "An Americano, with syrup?"

He shook his head side to side. "No. That's not what I want." His eyes never left the sign above. Not to acknowledge me, or the woman behind him.

"Sir," Jace stood over my shoulder, "Move to the side and let us help the next guest."

He looked at her with his eyes narrowed further, but he didn't say anything before stepping aside.

"How can I—"

"Give me a large Americano with vanilla syrup and cream." She handed me her card before I asked.

Before the next person could order, the unknown man took his place in front of me again. "Give me a large espresso with an extra shot of espresso, and skim milk."

I fumbled with the register as I tried to enter his order.

"Is there a problem?" he asked. I looked up and shook my head. But his eyes narrowed before I could look away.

I asked, "Can I have a name for the order?"

"Deshaun."

"It'll be right up," I said to him as I looked at the person behind him. He didn't move though. "Everything okay?"

His card outstretched toward me, and I clenched my eyes. "Unless for some reason my order is free."

"Unfortunately, not." I took his card and swiped it. "Have a great day," I said, handing it back to him. Still, he didn't move, and his eyes narrowed further.

The man behind him cleared his throat. "If that's over, I'd like to order."

As Deshaun moved to the side without responding, an

image flashed in my mind. *The elevator.* He was the guy I saw when I was leaving Bryer on my last day.

SIX

Deshaun

The woman behind the counter continued taking orders. She offered her smile to everyone who approached her. While I waited on my espresso, I found myself staring at her more than the rest of the people in line. Her pleasantries stopped sounding like nails on the chalkboard after she repeated them a few more times.

"Deshaun." The other woman behind the counter interrupted my thoughts. Good thing too. I didn't have time to admire the woman any longer.

I grabbed my cup and exited the shop.

"You're welcome," I heard shouted at my back, but continued.

From the café to my desk, I ran through my schedule for the afternoon. I had one more meeting with the department heads. Our discounts and insight weren't proving successful. It was time to recalibrate.

The receptionist had her head down when I exited the elevator. When she glanced up her mouth parted, but she snapped her lips shut. "Is Coco here?" I asked as I approached her.

I caught a look of panic in her eyes as if she wondered if that became her job to know Coco's whereabouts. Then she responded, "No, sir, Mr. Green. I haven't seen her this morning."

"Great," I said with a huff as I paced to my office. With my phone to my ear, I dialed Coco's number again. I'd called once that morning and it went to voicemail. In all the years I'd worked with Coco, she'd only missed work a handful of times. Each time she coordinated in advance and marked it on my calendar. With the phone ringing, I checked my calendar to be sure it wasn't an oversight on my part.

When it wasn't, I spoke into her voicemail. "Coco, I'm assuming something must have happened since you aren't in the office today. And not answering the phone." I hesitated with what to offer because I didn't know much about Coco outside of the office. I didn't know if she had a boyfriend, a group of friends, family in the area. I assumed most of them were back in New York. "If you need help. Let me know." I hung up the phone and placed it on my desk.

Without Coco in the office, someone else would need to capture the tasks for the next meeting. Outside of Coco though, there weren't many people I trusted to track the details.

I sat at my seat and rubbed a hand across my face. The move to Greensboro was starting to feel like more of a burden than an opportunity. If I didn't recover soon, I'd be looking for an exit plan.

The espresso I wasted time fetching was still in my hand when I opened my laptop. I took a sip and my face soured. "This is terrible." I groaned. If Coco was in the office, I would have had my order. *Could have taken the woman's request.*

I wasn't disturbed by the memory, instead her beautiful face offered a sense of peace. The woman was gorgeous. But it wasn't her looks that were most prevalent, it was the thought that I knew her from somewhere. I couldn't recall where. It wasn't like I visited the coffee shop often, and outside of work I wasn't doing much around the city. Not even the name on her apron jogged my memory.

A notification on my computer reminded me that I had no time to waste. Especially not trying to play twenty questions with my memory about a random woman.

"Mr. Green," I heard. Coco's voice was grasping for air as she stood at my door. "I'm here."

"After half the day is gone. Almost think it would have been better for you to stay home." I stood from my desk and walked toward her. "Since you're here, be ready to capture notes in this next meeting."

She followed behind me. "First it was my car, then my phone died..."

I wasn't interested in her excuses. I turned to her and said, "What happens outside of this office is not my concern."

"I heard your voicemail." Her voice was a whisper as we neared the conference room.

"You're here now," I said before entering. "Let's get right to it," I announced to the staff seated around the table.

Nate cleared his throat and stared at his computer screen

before he started speaking. "We have more customer feed-back." He adjusted his glasses. "The customers are complaining creative is not consistent with the old team. Some have stated Leah had a vision that differs from what we've produced."

"Leah?" Her name didn't stand out in the context. But it was the name of the woman in the coffee shop. "Nancy," I looked to the creative director, "Her notes should be in the files. Why aren't they referenced?" Nancy shifted in her seat before shuffling through a pile of papers in front of her. "Nancy?"

Her eyes snapped up to mine before she stuttered, "Well, I don't know."

I widened my stance then barked, "You don't know?" I slammed a fist onto the desk and shouted, "It's your job to know. Your team should be maintaining client expectations. Are you not talking to the clients? To your team?"

"Of course." She fidgeted with her fingers. "It seems Leah had a very detailed vision for most of the clients, and our team is having a hard time replicating it." Then she added, "Or any of the previous team."

My jaw tensed. Releasing the creative team felt like the right thing to do. At the time, with Bryer bleeding revenue, it wouldn't make sense to duplicate teams. Especially not when our creative team had managed every other acquisition with ease. "How is Bryer different from any other agency we've acquired?"

There were tight lips around the room. I wanted to release every department head in there. Fire them all and start from scratch, but finding new talent to replace them would take time. "Study those notes, determine how we can use them, and

I'll find this Leah woman." When nobody budged, I said, "Get back to work," before I walked out.

"You'll find her?" Coco was walking beside me trying to match my long stride. "How? And what makes you think she'll want to come back?"

"Employee files, Coco. I have all the information I need to find her."

"Oh, right. What can I do to help?"

I walked into my office and sat behind my desk. "Ask Benny to send me everything he has on Leah, and the rest of the old creative team."

"Got it." She rushed from my office.

Instead of scanning client files or emails, I turned to the windows and looked down at the city. There weren't honking cars or a rush of people on the sidewalk. The street wasn't lined with boutiques and bodegas. But there was a familiarity there in Greensboro. It was a building like the one I sat in that inspired me to pursue a degree in marketing. I wanted to sit in an office, high in the sky. Some would have said I made it. I accomplished my dreams, but if I couldn't turn Bryer around, it'd forever be a stain in my reputation.

"He's sent the files." Coco's voice was across the room. "What's next?"

"I find her."

"Leah Moore," she offered.

I sat at my desk and opened the email Benny sent. "Leah Moore," I repeated as the documents began to open. "She was with Bryer for ten years. Creative Manager." Then my words slowed as I read her latest performance review. "VP Promotion recommended," I hissed.

"What if she's already working for someone?"

"With her credentials and experience in this city." I groaned. "I can't imagine she isn't." I continued opening more files. I read her client list, her project summaries, then finally I opened her employee file. "It's her."

"Mr. Green?" Coco approached my desk. "What do you mean it's her?"

My eyes didn't leave my screen as I explained, "She's working right next door." Instead of explaining further, I turned the laptop screen around to show Coco the picture of Leah.

"She works at Cup of Sunshine." She paused. "How do you know that?"

I smirked and looked at the unfinished cup of coffee on my desk. "I had to fetch my own coffee today."

She cringed. "Sorry about that." After a minute, she offered, "But look. Now you've found her."

SEVEN

Leah

I pulled off my apron and sighed. "Have a good night." I looked at Jace as I walked around the counter. The extra steps made me wince.

"You okay?" She chuckled. "Still not used to standing on your feet all day, huh?"

I shook my head. "No." I leaned against the counter and stretched my ankle. "Not quite."

"At least you are on your way home. Soak in a nice bath." Jace's offer sounded like a good idea. If I were going home. Or if I was going to my own apartment where I could start a bath and light a few candles to relax. It was something I'd do after a long day at Bryer. I had no idea back then what a long day was, at least not physically.

I adjusted my purse strap and said, "I'm headed to the community center, so no long baths for me."

"After a day like today?" She tilted her head to the side. "Couldn't be me." She hunched her shoulders and turned to the back of the café as I walked out.

The walk to my car took me past the Bryer offices. The tall building had floors and floors of offices. Most of the lights were off and I imagined everyone was on their way home. If I were still there it was around the time I would have left. I stared for a few more minutes before I crossed the street and hopped into my car.

The gas light greeted me, and I dropped my head back to the seat. *Dear God, please let me have enough.* I shuffled through my purse and the tips I collected from the day. Pulling out each dollar and all the coins. "Twenty-five dollars and thirty-five cents." Enough to get me around until I got paid at the end of the week. "Thank you, God."

Before I pulled out of the parking spot, I glanced at the Bryer offices again. "There has to be something that comes from this," I whispered before driving away.

If I didn't have to stop for gas, I would have arrived to the center in time to help move food from the kitchen to the dining room. But I was a little late. I hurried to the dining room and squeezed into the serving line. "Hey," I said to one of the volunteers. I pulled gloves on and fell into serving each person as they passed. Although it felt like we served more than a hundred people that night, they moved along. My feet were thankful.

"You're not usually late." Ms. Carol stood in front of me with her head tilted as we cleared the dining tables.

I carried empty trays into the kitchen and explained, "Had to make a stop on my way here."

"Okay, was thinking you decided to take the night off for a date or something."

I laughed and shook my head. "Not tonight, Ms. Carol."

"Soon." She patted my shoulder as she started washing dishes.

"If only there was someone asking," I teased. But before she could suggest one of her many grandsons, I said, "I'm enjoying the time with myself."

She grumbled, "Baby, there's only so much alone time you need. Don't turn down all these men and miss out on your Boaz."

I held in my laugh and pointed over my shoulder. "I'm going to make sure we cleared everything." Others were walking in with their hands full, but I still escaped the kitchen.

"I'll help," I said to one of the volunteers moving a table into a corner. The small community center wasn't anything fancy. The folding chairs and banquet tables had seen better days. There wasn't much space to move around. But with a few volunteers we were able to get the space back into its original state. I couldn't exactly say clean. Even with our efforts there wasn't much we could do about the tattered walls and missing paint.

"I heard Ms. Carol asking you about a date." Michelle was standing on the other side of the room. "As soon as I heard her ask, I eased away from the kitchen." She laughed. "She drilled me the last time I was here."

"If only that was something I worried about right now."

Michelle pointed to me. "I mean," she wagged her head, "I won't say I'm not worried about it." She walked across the room then looked over her shoulder. "But let's say the guy I've been looking at happens to be here."

My eyes widened. "Here?" There were a few men who volunteered. A couple were there that night even. Outside of volunteers there were the members we were serving. "Who?"

She grit her teeth before saying, "Your brother."

I gasped and put a hand on my chest. "As in Liam?" Of course, she was talking about Liam. He was my one and only brother, but I didn't find many women who were falling for him. "Have you talked to him?" I laughed.

"No." She shook her head. "I was hoping he'd talk to me. Been coming in here for weeks now."

"For him?" I laughed again. But when her face remained stoic, I said, "Oh. Okay. I can drop a hint for him if you'd like."

"See, that's what I'm talking about." She wrapped an arm around my shoulder.

"I'm headed to his office now." I winked.

If it weren't for my aching feet, I would have wanted to skip to Liam's office. As far as I knew, Liam wasn't dating anyone. Unlike me, he could have time for a love life. And what I knew about Michelle, she seemed like a good match.

By the time I walked down the long, narrow hallway and stood in front of Liam's office, I had a wide smile on my face. "Liam," I blurted when I walked through the door. "Guess what?"

"You talked to Dad?"

My eyes narrowed and I turned my head to the side. "No." Then I corrected. "Well, yes. I live with them. So yes, we talked this morning." My smile started to fade when his mouth turned into a frown. "What happened?"

"He called this morning saying that the property tax bill was due, and they may not be able to pay it."

"What?" I looked over his head. That morning before leaving, I saw my dad in the kitchen. He was in his usual grumpy morning mood but didn't mention anything about a property tax bill. "Was he asking for help to pay it?"

Liam's focus was on a stack of papers in front of him. "No. But I mean." He looked up to me. "I offered. What little I have to spare anyway." His chuckle came out, almost nervously. "Seems like when it rains it pours around here, huh?"

"Yeah," I mumbled. "I guess you could say that." For me it was more like a torrential downpour with hurricane force winds. I was standing in the middle of it as my umbrella flew out of my hands. "I'm not making their situation any easier."

He removed his glasses and said, "It's not like that." He stood from his seat and stretched his arms over his head. "We could all use a little more help." He looked up to the ceiling. "A few blessings if you have them to spare, God." He laughed. "Even this place." He picked up a pen and dropped it. "We have more members than we have beds for another night." He groaned.

"Guess I shouldn't tell you this place could use a fresh paint then, huh?" My nose crinkled as I plucked at my shirt.

"Only if you have time to paint, and money to buy it."

I laughed. "In that case, I have something else to share."

"What's up?"

"Well..." My body swiveled back and forth like I was on the playground talking to a crush of my own. I laughed. "I don't know why I'm nervous like it has anything to do with me."

"Nervous?"

"Michelle," I blurted. "The volunteer. She might have a little crush on you."

Liam's eyes widened. "See. God coming through already. She's fine." He rubbed his hands together.

"Hopefully, that's only the beginning. Make sure you speak to her before you leave." I waved my hand and turned toward the door. "I better get out of here. I need to find a second job. Or a better paying first job."

"Hey..." Liam walked out from behind his desk. "It'll all work out."

"It will," I told him. As his older sister I felt like I should be the one with the encouraging words. The confidence that everything would be okay. Although I was saying it, I didn't quite feel it.

I felt it even less as I pulled into the driveway of my parents' house. Only the kitchen light was on, and I made my way toward it. My mom was at the counter sipping from a mug. "Hey, Mama." I wrapped my arm around her shoulders. I held on a little longer when I felt her shoulders slump and her chest heave. "Everything okay?"

The wrinkles in her skin were defined. The grays around her edges filling in more. Before that night, I'm not sure I recognized it.

"I'm okay, baby." Her smile hardly lifted her eyes.

"I talked to Liam, said Dad called him earlier today. Why didn't anyone tell me about the tax bill?" I looked over my shoulder. "I saw Dad this morning."

"You have enough on your plate. I told him not to worry you."

"But," I shook my head, "If you two are having financial issues, me being here isn't helping."

She placed a hand over mine. "Leah, we've been in situations like this before. Your dad," she sighed before she changed directions, "don't worry about all that. He'll figure it out. I promise."

"And I'll do my part to figure something out." I assured her, "I've been looking. But I'm going to put that into overdrive."

"Do what's best for you." She smiled. "And we'll figure out our situation." I hugged her again before I walked back to my room.

Sitting on the floor against my daybed, I pulled out my phone. *There had to be somewhere else I could work.* I scrolled through pages and pages of positions. I applied to as many as possible before my eyes grew heavy, and it was time for me to get ready for bed.

EIGHT

Deshaun

I'd been dodging my parents' invite to dinner for a few months. It was finally time to sit down with them. My mama had called for a week straight reminding me of the day. She even assured me my siblings wouldn't be around to pester me. That part was the icing on the cake. I didn't need to hear them complain about their manufactured problems.

Holding my knuckles to the door instead of walking straight in felt strange. It was the same door I busted through many times as a kid. I took a deep breath and raised my fist to knock anyway.

My mom's opened arms embraced me as soon as the door flung open. Almost as if she hadn't seen me in years. "Deshaun, it's so good to see you," she whispered into my ear before pulling away. She kept my hand in hers as she scanned

my body. "You look like you need a good homecooked meal."
Then she laughed. "You're back home now, you know you
could drop into any of the restaurants to grab a plate during
the week."

I smirked. "Mom, you know I try to maintain my
physique." I posed for her.

Her other hand flew toward my shoulder, but I ducked
before it connected. "Boy, we raised you on that food."

"Whatever is in there smells good though," I said, walking
toward the kitchen.

"I made an extra special meal for you tonight." She was
walking behind me as she listed off the food I hadn't eaten in
over a year. "Greens, black-eyed peas, rice, stewed chicken,
cornbread, and candied yams."

A loud grumble left my stomach. I rubbed it as I said, "I
can't lie, sounds delicious."

The kitchen counter didn't have any serving dishes or
plates on it. But we could have all comfortably sat there.
"Where's all the food?" I turned behind me. Mom wasn't
there.

I heard, "In here, Deshaun," from the other room.

I walked into the dining room, where the food was spread
across the table like it was a holiday. My dad stood at the head
of the table as I entered. His arms outstretched. "It's about
time, son." He patted my back then said, "Your mama told me
you've been too busy to come and break bread with your
folks." He frowned as I found a seat at the table.

"It's not that I didn't want to be here, but the new agency
has kept me busy." I prepared my plate and told them, "This
looks good though." The aroma from the food brought me back

to my childhood. When they used our kitchen to test out the meals that would end up on the menu. We were the original taste testers. "I've missed your food, Mama," I said, looking over at her.

She sipped from her glass of wine before nodding. "To think, you are only down the street and haven't stopped by." Her head wagged side to side. "Unlike Bianca and Davion, those two can't seem to find anywhere else to eat. In fact, they grumbled about not being able to come over tonight."

I shook my head. "I can imagine they take advantage of it."

"That's not all they take advantage of." My dad's face turned into a scowl. "Those two could use some mentorship."

My eyes turned downward. I was hoping to avoid the inevitable conversation about the two of them. When my parents realized I wasn't coming back to run the family business after college, they pleaded with me. Told me to at least come back long enough to train my brother and sister, but I had bigger dreams. I wanted to start my own legacy.

"I could say it's because you spoiled them." Bianca was older than me, but she suffered from being the first child and grandchild in the family. Then Davion, he was the youngest, so by default he was rotten. Then there was me. The one in the middle who had to stand out. "I'd think after a master's in business, Bianca could dominate the company."

My mama stopped my dad from complaining with her hand raised. "I told them not to come tonight so that this wouldn't happen. Let's enjoy each other without talking about business."

I didn't mind that approach at all. Not talking about business was a good enough distraction from what I knew they wanted to discuss. Their retirement. It had been lingering for months.

"How has it been moving home?" My mom's voice had softened. "I assume not much has changed."

I placed my fork down and said, "Not too much. I can still navigate with ease. Most of the places I frequented before I left for college are still around. Southern hospitality is still intact." I smirked.

"That's what makes this place great." My mama had a smile on her face. "And what about your romantic life?"

The only other topic I wanted to discuss less than their retirement. "You mean the non-existent one?" I hunched my shoulders. "I don't have time."

My dad placed his fork down and sat back in his chair. "Don't have time for a good meal. Or to visit your family. Don't have time for a good woman." His arms went over his chest. "Doesn't sound sustainable to me."

"I would have to agree, honey." My mama dabbed her napkin against her mouth. "Look at me and your father. We've been able to have a good balance between the business and the family all these years." Her eyes narrowed as she stared down her nose at me. "Unless you don't agree you had enough attention from us growing up."

That was a challenge I wasn't about to accept. There was no way I was about to tell my parents they didn't do the best at raising us. "Of course not. You two raised us well." I elaborated even more. "You made sure we had everything we needed. Let us get most of what we wanted. Made sure we had home-cooked meals throughout the week."

"It wasn't easy." Mama looked at my dad. "We had to sacrifice time from ourselves to make sure we made time for the three of you."

My dad reached for her hand. "But ask us if we'd do it all over again. Now that it's time for us to retire, we will be able to enjoy the fruits of our labor."

I eyed the two of them. "That was a great segue." I joked, "Almost like you planned it." I sneered.

"We know that you'd be great leading the company. It'd be a great transition. Only until Bianca and Davion can get the hang of things." My dad's hand left my mom's as he rubbed it over his face. His beard no longer a deep black, but gray all over.

"But..." I looked between the two of them. "If I don't have time now for my own businesses, how do you expect I'd be able to pick up another?"

"We are hoping you've planned a better succession plan. That you have someone primed and ready to take the helm while you are away." My mom's confidence in my planning was hardcore. "I can't imagine the transition would be longer than six months, unless you decide to stay longer." She smiled as she said it.

"Unfortunately..." I hadn't planned to tell them that Bryer was doing bad. I didn't want them to think I put in all that effort only for it to be failing. "Bryer isn't performing as I expected it to. I can't leave right now. Even if I did have someone ready to take the wheel."

A pained look crossed my dad's face, and I couldn't bear to look Mama's way. The disappointment that would be staring at me would be hard to stomach.

"What's going on?" she asked.

"When I acquired the company, I released the creative

department. Our creative team is large and can take on the new projects. Except, the Bryer clients have been pushing back. They don't like the direction of my team."

I recoiled as I waited on the advice that was sure to follow my explanation. Our businesses varied greatly. But Dad never missed an opportunity to give me his two cents.

"You released the entire team?" My dad shifted in his seat. "After they transitioned to your team, right?"

I shook my head. "Not exactly. Our team takes over from day one."

"Imagine hiring a full staff at a restaurant and expecting them to run things without being trained on our menu." He was looking at my mom. "Can't imagine that location would be successful. But if that's what you've always done, why do you think it's not working?"

"There seems to be someone on the old team that most of the clients favor. For whatever reason, our team cannot replicate her vision."

"So, she's the cookbook holding Bryer's secret recipes. And she was dismissed without question?" My dad's head nodded as if he was pulling all the pieces together. "Sounds like you need to bring her back."

That was in the works. Bringing Leah and the rest of the team back was my highest priority. "That's what I plan to do."

He leaned over and patted my back. "See son, you know what you need to do." He laughed. "Not sure Bianca or Davion would come to that same conclusion."

Always defending the two of them, Mama said, "I also don't know if they would have fired the team in the first place." She took another sip of her wine and peered at me over the brim. "It's good you are correcting your wrongs. It'd be wiser to be more cautious going forward. Even with our chain of restaurants, we accepted that everything doesn't work everywhere. Sometimes you need to adjust."

"Hard lesson, but I've learned it," I assured her.

"Good, we expect you'll resolve everything with Bryer. Then we can revisit this conversation about retirement." My dad stood from his seat. "Jocelyn, how about some of your poundcake?"

NINE

Leah

With heavy eyelids, I rushed through my morning routine. If I was lucky, I could pick up a few deliveries on the way into work. Becoming a food delivery driver was the quickest way to earn extra money. Except, it meant that I was working longer hours.

I took a cold towel to my face, and prayed, "Dear God, give me the strength to make it through this day." I tossed the towel into the hamper as I plucked a black shirt and slacks from my closet. "I got this," I whispered.

I had one arm in my shirt when my phone started ringing. The unknown number on the screen was almost ignored, then something told me to answer. I finished pulling the shirt over my head and said, "Hello?" as the phone cradled on my shoulder.

The robotic recording I expected to respond wasn't there. I

didn't hear, "Your car warranty has expired, and we can offer you an extension."

Instead, it was a soft voice that asked, "Ms. Moore?"

I leaned against the bed and replied, "Yes, this is Ms. Moore."

"Ah, perfect. I was hoping I'd catch you. I apologize for the early call. This is Shelby Lee from Brown Brothers Marketing Agency."

My eyes widened as I straightened. I'd submitted my resume to their agency months ago. Even with disapproval from Kerry, I had to try all agencies in the city.

"We'd love to interview you for a position here at the agency."

I couldn't believe what I was hearing and had to blink a few times to make sure I wasn't delusional. I put a hand up to my head and pat the curls I needed to be pull into a ponytail.

"Okay," I said. "That's great."

"If possible, we'd like for you to come in at nine o'clock."

"I'd love to," I told her, "And that's nine o'clock on which date, I'm sorry, I missed it." I pulled the phone closer to my ear to ensure I didn't miss any details. Then I scoured the nightstand for a pen and paper.

She hesitated before she answered, "Today." Then apologized. "I know it's terrible notice, but Jacob has limited availability."

Jacob Brown. Of the *Brown Brothers Marketing Agency.* Even when I interviewed at Bryer, it was months before I met Mr. Bryer himself. He made his presence known around the office without us seeing him.

Was there another Jacob at the agency? As a family business, there could be more than one, right? *A junior, and a senior?* "Jacob Brown?" I asked.

"Yes, I hope that's okay. Typically, he isn't the one doing the interviews. But he'd like to meet with you. Today at nine o'clock," she repeated.

Nine o'clock, when I should be at *Cup of Sunshine.* "Goodness, I was on my way to work," I said to myself more than to her. *I need to change clothes, do something with my hair.*

"If it's at all possible, I suggest you do whatever you can to make this happen. He'd be very appreciative of your time, and I'll inform him it's limited."

Although I didn't respond as quick, I was nodding my head. "I'll be there," I said. "Nine o'clock." My chest was heaving as I thought about the questions he could ask. Or if I could even recall my project work. *God, please help me.*

Shelby continued giving me instructions for my arrival. After she hung up, I ran to my closet to find something other than the black t-shirt and pants I planned to wear that day.

My suits were scrunched to the back of the closet. I had to shuffle through the basic t-shirts and pants that had become my daily attire to get to them. Then I had to find a pair of pumps. That didn't take long. With only two pairs that would fit in the small closet, I didn't have many options. I snatched up the brown pair and my blue suit, then rushed into the bathroom.

"Wearing a suit today?" my mom asked as I passed her.

"Yes," I said, "something like that. I'll explain later," before closing the door. Pulling the jacket on made me feel like myself again. Like I was ready to conquer the world.

On my way out of the house, I passed my dad in the

kitchen. For the first time in months, he had a slither of a smile on his face as he said, "This looks promising."

"I hope so," I told him as I rushed to the front door.

As I drove, I called into work and let them know I'd be running a little late. Jace answered and said, "Okay, see you when you get here," with little enthusiasm.

My hands were wringing around the steering wheel as I navigated traffic. All I could repeat was, "God, please let me arrive on time." Then as I pulled into the parking spot, with ten minutes to spare, I uttered, "Thank you," before stepping out.

I entered the lobby and smoothed my hands over my pants. At the security desk I announced, "I'm here for an interview with the Brown Brothers Agency." The security guard escorted me to the elevator and hit the button for the tenth floor.

When the doors opened, I picked at my shirt. The layer of sweat that transpired made it stick to my skin. I looked down and hoped my jacket would cover any signs of my nerves.

"Ms. Moore," I heard as I approached the receptionist's desk. A woman appeared with a beautiful smile and a wave. She outstretched her hand and said, "I'm Shelby, we spoke on the phone."

"Of course." I shook her hand. "I recognize your voice."

The office wasn't much like Bryer. It had a masculine touch to it. A dark wood receptionist desk with a heavy steel *Brown Brothers Agency* sign behind it.

"I'll take you right on in," Shelby said as she walked toward a glass door. Behind it were more dark wooden desks. Each person we passed was either concentrating on a laptop or had a phone to their ear. "This is our main floor, and we have one that mirrors it above," her eyes went up, "and below," then down.

"How large is the creative team?" The team at Bryer was under thirty. From the looks of it, Brown Brothers had a larger presence.

"Great question." She tapped her chin. "The total team is now upward of one hundred. Larger than Bryer, right?"

I nodded. "About triple the size."

"It won't feel like it. We're like family here." She winked as she placed her hand on an oversized wooden door. "Right this way."

I stepped into the office after her and the sheer size of the space amazed me. It was expansive, with a sitting area, a conference table, and a desk. Shelby started speaking again as my eyes found the man seated behind it. "Mr. Brown," Shelby's eyes bounced between me and him, "Ms. Leah Moore." Then in a whisper, she emphasized, "And she has a hard thirty-minute stop." She looked at me. "I'll be back in thirty."

As she walked out, I remained standing in front of the desk. The sweat dripping down my back made more apparent as Mr. Brown's eyes scanned my body.

"Please have a seat." His hand outstretched.

As I sat, I said, "Thank you for this opportunity, Mr. Brown." I crossed my legs and eased into the seat. I was ready to provide examples of projects I worked on, projects I led, and the success I had with my clients.

"I understand your experience. Bryer being one of our competitors, some of my staff have bid against you for projects." His face was stoic as he continued. "With the acquisition, I'd think the creative team would be the last to go."

I gulped as a lump formed in my throat.

"It's okay," he said. "You can agree." His lips spread into a thin smile. "I'd like to think we take a more strategic approach here at Brown Brothers."

"As a marketing agency, I'd like to think the creative department is the bread and butter." My back straightened. While at Bryer, it was our team who received most of the recognition.

Mr. Brown pointed with a wide smile. "Exactly. Ms. Moore, I know you have limited time. Usually, I'd send you through a barrage of questions. I like to know anyone we bring on our team can perform." He bit the side of his mouth. "But your reputation precedes you. I heard it was your talent that sustained many clients at Bryer. With you on our team, I suspect you'll be as successful."

"I had an amazing team there." I knew I could deliver, but starting with a new team did make me nervous.

"Our team is amazing." Mr. Brown's smile widened. "If you aren't pursuing another agency, I'd love for you to join them." He looked at his watch and said, "And I can give you back fifteen minutes of your time."

It was nothing like my interview with Bryer. There I sat through three rounds of interviews with a panel of people. "That's it?"

He laughed again. "Continue building that desirable rapport with clients. Any agency in this city would be clamoring at the opportunity to have you."

I stopped my mouth from tensing. If he only knew, of all the agencies I contacted, his was the only one who interviewed me. *That's not important.* "Thank you."

Then he told me, "If we are fortunate for you to join us, I guarantee we'll make the terms worthy. Better than what you had at Bryer." He smirked. "I heard Bryer held his purse strings a little tight. Around here, we pride ourselves in respecting our staff." He stood, looking at his watch again as he did. "What do you say? Check out what we have to offer and let us know this evening if it's acceptable."

His hand outstretched in front of me again. I shook it and responded, "I can do that."

Walking to his office door, there was a joy bubbling up within me. I wanted to shout, "Glory to God." But settled for a whispered, "Thank you, Jesus." I was in awe as Shelby greeted me.

"This is for you." She handed me a folder. "Inside you'll find your offer letter. An explanation of benefits, and," she smiled a little wider, "perks."

Her hand dangled for a minute before I took the folder. "I'm sorry," I told her, "This all happened so fast."

She shrugged. "Mr. Brown doesn't like to waste any time. I hope to see you around."

On my way to Cup of Sunshine, I called Janine. When she answered, I screamed, "I was offered a job at Brown Brothers Marketing Agency."

"Wait, what?"

Saying it out loud felt even more unbelievable. My heart was racing, and my skin felt like it was vibrating. "I was offered a job at Brown Brothers Marketing Agency."

She was screaming as loud as I was when she said, "That's my girl. I told you everything would work out for you."

"And it's more than what I was making at Bryer." I hadn't reviewed the *perks*, but knowing they were in my package, I said, "And there are perks."

"Look at God."

I was smiling until I said, "It was a strange interview though. I interviewed with one of the co-founders. And he didn't ask me anything about my experience."

"Oh." Janine paused. "That is weird. But if you got the job, I guess it doesn't matter. Tell me you are going to take this job."

"Of course." As I parked my car beside the café, I said, "I just need to give my two weeks' notice."

Janine laughed. "Always the saint."

I was getting out of the car with my bag to change clothes when I said, "I better run. Gotta get into work now."

"Leah," she said before I could hang up, "I'm proud of you."

"Thanks, Janine."

I ran across the street and tried to make it to the bathroom. Behind me, I heard someone call out my name.

TEN

Deshaun

"Coco," I shouted.

She ran into my office with her tablet balanced on her hip. "Is it necessary for you to scream my name? You know," she pointed to the phone on my desk, "You can pick that up and call me." Then she pointed to the cell in my hand, "Or text me with that. The shouting startles everyone around."

"That's not my concern," I told her. "It's quicker for me to get you in here."

She adjusted her stance. "How can I help you?" She clenched her jaw and didn't smile.

"Where are you with contacting the rest of the creative team?" Last I checked, half of the team was already prepared to onboard. "What's the hold up?"

"Benny has contacted everyone and is negotiating salaries and details." Her eyebrows pinched together. "Except for

Leah." Her head swiveled from me to the bookcase beside me. "I'm not sure she's responded to his calls."

"She's right next door." I pointed my hand toward the window. "Why hasn't someone walked over and asked her? What part of she's vital to the clients doesn't anyone understand?" I was standing from my desk, walking toward the windows. "How hard can it be to get her to come back? I mean, she's working at a coffee shop. Can't imagine she wouldn't want to come back."

"Right. So, you'd like *me* to talk to her?" There was a smirk on Coco's face that wasn't there before I looked out the window.

"No," I told her. Then I thought about who the best person would be to approach her. "You know what? I'll do it."

"You'll do it?" Coco's voice screeched. "Like *you* are going to go into the coffee shop and ask her to return to Bryer?"

I pulled my jacket off, rolled up my sleeves, and told her, "Yes."

She tugged on her earlobe. "Seems like something someone else should be doing. Or we should wait until she answers. Is it not intrusive to show up at her job and offer her another? Especially after you fired her?"

Coco's rambling started to irritate me. I walked past her to the door and said, "I'll be back."

Walking through the office and riding down the elevator, I toyed with the words I'd say to her. Desperation wouldn't look good on me, and I'd never pleaded for anything in my life. But if she was the lifeline I needed to save Bryer, I was willing to compromise.

I expected to see her behind the counter when I walked into the café, but as I craned my neck, I didn't see her. If she wasn't there, that'd mess up my plan. I needed her back at Bryer ASAP. The door opened behind me, and a woman rushed by.

She wasn't wearing a t-shirt and slacks though. She had on a suit and pumps. Her face tilted toward mine, and before I could stop myself, her name rolled off my tongue, "Leah?"

I walked the few steps between us and said, "Are you working today?"

A bag dangled from her hand, and she said, "Yes, trying to." She bit the side of her mouth. "I need to change my clothes."

"If you have a minute, I wanted to discuss something with you."

The line behind me was growing and she cringed. "I should at least change my clothes. They need my help."

There was an empty seat beside me. "Okay," I told her. "I'll be waiting here when you catch a minute."

She continued to the bathroom, and I took a seat. My phone vibrated and I answered, "Yes?"

"Mr. Green, you have a meeting in fifteen minutes," Coco said.

I looked at my watch and told her, "Push it out to this afternoon. I need to handle this first."

"Right," she said. "Got it."

I expected Leah would return to me after she changed clothes. She didn't. It wasn't until she served the entire line and there weren't many other people in the café.

"You needed to discuss something?" She handed me a cup.

"What is this?" I asked.

"An espresso with an extra shot of espresso, and skim milk," she said, "Sorry to keep you waiting." I noticed her the last time, but sitting in front of me her beauty was captivating. There was something behind her eyes that didn't let me look away. And her smile, each time it spread across her face something tugged in my chest.

"Oh." I placed it in front of me. "That wasn't exactly the right order last time."

A frown replaced her smile. "I can make the right order." She smirked. "If you remember it." The frown wasn't as pretty. Nowhere near as captivating.

"This is fine," I told her, "Thanks." I shifted in the seat. Sitting there for an hour was starting to make me regret my decision to wait on her.

"Of course." The door opened and she watched another person approach the counter.

"I'll be quick," I said, "I am Deshaun Green. The CEO of Bryer."

Her eyes looked panicked as she said, "I'm beyond the six-month non-compete."

"I'm sorry, what?"

"Are you here because I interviewed with the Brown Brothers?" She leaned forward.

"You did?" The coffee was horrible the first time I had it, but I needed anything to moisten my mouth, so I took a sip. "I wasn't here about that. I was coming to inform you that I've asked the creative team to rejoin the company. We've tried to contact you, but had no success. And I would like to extend an offer to you. I can have HR call you with all the details."

Her arms went across her chest. "Really?" She shook her head. "I don't know what to say."

"I hope you'll say you'll return to Bryer, and not go to the competition."

Brown Brothers was already beating us with new clients. Some of our existing clients were jumping ship to join them. If Leah joined their team, it wouldn't be long before other clients followed.

"I need to get back to work. If HR has something to present, they can email me." She stood from the chair, and I followed. "Should be in my employee file."

"Right," I told her with my hand outstretched. "Thank you for taking a minute." Her hand rested in mine, and our eyes connected. "I hope to hear from you soon." I should have released her hand, but I didn't.

"I need that hand to pour coffee." She laughed.

"Right, of course." I dropped her hand and stuck mine in my pocket. "Have a good day." I watched as she walked back to the counter.

Jacob offered her a job? I walked back to the office and told Coco as soon as I saw her, "Tell Benny to email Leah an offer."

Her eyes widened before she said, "Sure."

I closed the door behind me and called Jacob. He sounded cheerful when he answered, "Mr. Green, how are you doing today, sir?" Much more cheerful than he would on any other day.

"Great." I stood in front of my bookcase. "I have to admit, I didn't think returning to Greensboro would mean the two of us would be at odds in any way though."

He chuckled into the phone. "You and me? At odds? How is that?"

"I hear you are hiring one of Bryer's finest."

He sucked his teeth. "Fine she is."

I rubbed a hand across my beard. It wasn't unlike him to be

unprofessional. But for some reason, it rubbed me the wrong way.

"If I'm not mistaken, she's no longer a Bryer employee, correct?" he said with an unsettling tone. "One you, yourself, fired?"

My hand gripped my tie, and I loosened it. "A mistake I can admit. We are bringing the team back though."

"Oh," he said, "are you?" Then he offered, "Well, good luck on that." He laughed a little harder. "What's that you said when you moved to the city, 'may the best man win'? Oh, and tell Coco I said hello."

He sent my blood boiling.

ELEVEN

Leah

The afternoon rush was over, and I had time to sit down and review the offer from the Brown Brothers Agency. I sat near the window, reading through each line of the letter. I read through the line with my salary details a few times. Tears formed in my eyes when I looked up to the ceiling. "God, this is better than anything I could have imagined."

Of course, losing my job was the lowest of lows. But if the way I was bouncing back was the result, it took some of the sting out of it. Not only was the salary outstanding, so were the perks. "Paid vacation, paid healthcare, an annual company trip." When I read it, I had to swipe the tear from my face. I didn't let any of it deter me from reading the rest, and by the time I finished I was ready to sign.

I sat back in my seat though. There was Mr. Green's offer to return to Bryer to consider. I dug my phone from my back pocket and scrolled through my emails until I found an email from Benny. The salary didn't compare to the offer from Bryer. *Mr. Bryer wasn't the only one tight on the purse strings. It was Mr. Green too.*

Before I did anything else, I closed my eyes and bowed my head. "Dear, God, thank you for not one offer, but two. Thank you for sustaining me up until now. Please lead me to the right decision." Before I finished, I heard the chime from the front door. "Amen," I whispered as I opened my eyes.

Mr. Green was walking into the café again. He neared the counter, and Jace pointed to the corner where I sat. "Mr. Green," I said as he approached. "Can I help you?"

"Hear me out," he said with his hands outstretched. "I understand you have two offers to consider."

It was already decided, but his words were coming too fast for me to interrupt him.

"Allow me to take you out to dinner tonight."

My head jerked back. "Why would you do that?"

"I realize returning to Bryer may present challenges. I want the opportunity to discuss my vision for Bryer with you." He paused and stood with his hands near his sides.

Instead of straining my neck to look up at him, I stood from my seat. "I don't think that's necessary." I shook my head. "I have both offers. And," I didn't want to tell him I had already decided, so I settled on saying, "I'll consider both and let Benny know either way."

"Anywhere you'd like."

"I'm sorry?"

"Any place in the city, you name it."

It had been a while since I was able to enjoy a night out. Getting dressed for a nice dinner did sound appealing. "Okay,"

I sighed. "If you insist." Then I felt bad for accepting the invite knowing I planned to accept the offer from Brown Brothers. "But, I should tell you, I've decided to take the offer from Brown Brothers."

His jaw twitched, and his chest heaved. "Allow me the opportunity to change your mind."

I hunched my shoulders and pulled my phone from my pocket. "I can be ready by eight," I told him as I unlocked the phone. "If you give me a number, I can let you know what place I'll meet you at."

"Meet me." He fidgeted with his pocket before pulling his own phone out. "Of course." After giving me his number, he asked for mine. "I'll be expecting a call." He walked out, and I stood watching.

"What was that?" I heard from the back of the store. "Is that Leah getting a man?"

My cheeks warmed as Jace continued. "No, that is Leah..." I hesitated. I hadn't submitted my resignation and didn't want to broadcast that I was quitting yet. I hurried to the counter and said, "It's Leah getting back to her career," under my breath.

"With a coworker like that I need to consider a change of jobs. Think they'll hire me?" Her eyes were on the front door.

Only two dresses appropriate for dinner hung in my closet. Deciding between the two was easy. One was a little black dress I'd wear if I was going out on a date. The other, was something I'd worn in the office a few times. I went with that one.

But as I stood in front of the hostess stand at the steak house, I was thinking I could have gone with the black one. The steak house was nice, and everyone around me dressed for a date. Not a meeting in the conference room.

The hostess asked, "Reservations?"

I grit my teeth. "No, I didn't make reservations. But I'm meeting Mr. Green, the reservations could be under his name." I hoped he did as I looked at the tables. Not many were empty.

"Ah, yes." She sat the menu in her hand on the podium and told me, "He's already here. Right this way." I followed behind her, through the restaurant to the back. "Mr. Green," she announced after opening a door. "Your guest has arrived."

"Ms. Moore," he said, standing. "Glad you made it okay." The suit he was wearing was different than the shirt and slacks he had on earlier that day. He looked nice with a tie around his neck, jacket over his torso, but I liked the casual look on him too.

The hostess left us alone and I found a seat before he helped me scoot in. "A private room." I looked over my shoulder as he sat across from me. "Will we be discussing secret matters tonight?"

He sneered. "Not exactly. Whenever possible, I like to dine away from anyone else."

I grabbed the glass of water on the table and said, "I see," before taking a sip. There wasn't a menu on the table, and I said, "I haven't been here before."

"They'll bring a menu for you to look at. I assumed if you suggested it, you already had an idea of what you wanted to eat."

I shook my head. "Not exactly."

There was a server at our table within minutes handing us menus and waiting for our orders. After we ordered, Mr. Green said, "Our clients have nothing but good things to say about you."

"That's good to hear. Before the acquisition I was being considered for a VP position." The role at Brown Brothers would have been an associate. I didn't want to have to work up the ladder. It took years for me to get into the management role, and starting as an associate again felt like a loss in a way. Even with a salary increase.

"I see. We can offer you the same position," he said it without hesitation. "I'd prefer to see you on our team."

"And match the Brown Brothers salary?"

"Well..." He tugged on his tie. "That depends." I gave him the number and his eyes bulged. "I need to run that by our HR department." The server returned with appetizers, and Mr. Green offered, "I can get that to you as soon as we leave. So, the coffee shop?"

"The coffee shop?" I repeated before lifting a finger and bowing my head. I recited a prayer to myself.

When I opened my eyes he was staring at me. "Were you unable to find a position at another agency?"

I shook my head. "Not a single one." Then I smiled. "Now two in one day."

His eyes fell downward. "Ms. Moore—"

"Feel free to call me Leah."

"Leah," he cleared his throat, "I hope you know the decision to let you go was not personal. It didn't reflect your skillset, or your effort at Bryer."

I didn't believe it did, still it was good to hear him confirm. "For months I've tried to understand why this happened. I can only imagine when it's all said and done, I'll look back and understand God's plan."

"God's plan." He placed his fork down. "I take it you are religious."

It wasn't a secret. Not something I was willing to hide. "I am." I didn't question his beliefs or elaborate.

All he said in response was, "Okay." After our entrées were served he shared, "My mom is in church every Sunday."

"I try to be." Then I tilted my head to the side and asked, "Do you not attend church?"

He shook his head. "Not since I was a kid and my parents forced me."

The steak I ordered was perfectly cooked, still I only had a few bites. I pushed around the mashed potatoes and the broccolini. "You said you wanted to discuss your vision," I reminded him. "Of Bryer."

He relaxed in his seat and wrapped his hand around his glass. He didn't raise it to his mouth though. "I have agencies in major cities, notable clients. The goal is to raise Bryer to the caliber of those agencies. Greensboro may not be a city on the map when discussing marketing agencies, but I'd like that to change."

As he continued, my eyebrows raised, and I eased into my seat.

"I hoped to have Bryer in the green within six months. But—"

"It's not?"

He took a long sip of his drink. "It's not. I still think it's possible though."

The moisture on his lips reminded me that my throat was

dry. I drank the remaining water in my glass and looked around for the server. "I could use a refill."

Mr. Green raised his hand, and there appeared a server at our table with the pitcher of water. My eyes narrowed as I looked at Mr. Green. "If I were still there, I would have been on board with helping you reach your vision for Bryer." I explained, "If I return, or not, I hope that you can achieve everything you hope."

TWELVE

Deshaun

Ms. Leah Moore has declined the offer. I sat at my desk reading the message from Benny on my laptop. It wasn't what I expected to see first thing in the morning. After the dinner I had with her I thought she was going to accept.

"It's fine, the rest of the team is here," I said to myself before I heard a knock at the door. "Come in," I shouted.

Coco stood in front of me with her eyes bulging. "Mr. Green..."

I didn't need the theatrics and raised from my seat to remind her of that.

"We have a problem."

The muscles in my neck tensed, and I rubbed my temples. "At least one thing is consistent around here," I grumbled. "What is it, Coco?"

"Our network is down." She tapped on her screen a few times. "And nobody can access the client files."

I sat down, typed into my computer, and attempted to open the Bryer folders. "But I can see all the other files. It's only the Bryer files."

"Right."

"Okay, so who is on it?" Bryer had an IT person in the office, and we had a team of experts across all the agencies. "Someone should be able to resolve this promptly."

She bit the side of her lip. "That's just it. They've been working on it all morning."

"All morning? And I'm only hearing about it now?" I felt my chest tightening. "Who do we need to call?" As I asked her, I realized she wouldn't have the answers I needed. I started to walk to the other side of the office, where the IT guy sat. "Don't worry about it, Coco, I'll talk to Brian."

"What should I do?"

I snapped, "Whatever it is you usually do in the morning."

When I reached Brian's office, I opened the door and adjusted my eyes to the darkness and illuminated lights coming from his machine. "Brian?" I'd only spoken to him a few times over the months I'd been in the office. He was a guy of few words but guaranteed me he knew his job. "What is going on?" I asked when his eyes left his screen.

"Mr. Green," he said as he typed. "There was a breach in the network. Our security measures are to shut down the system to prevent the loss of information."

"Security measures? Our security measures are preventing those who should have access to view files." I didn't need to elaborate on why that was a problem.

"Right."

"How soon can you resolve this?"

"As soon as possible." He was tapping away at the keyboard like he was playing a composition on the piano.

"If you need help, whatever you need, let me know. I need this resolved within the hour."

His tapping stopped and his eyes met mine. I walked out before hearing him reply.

Before I could even make it to my office, my phone was vibrating in my pocket. Bianca's name on the screen caught me off guard. She hardly ever called me, especially not in the middle of the work week. The last thing I needed was another problem. I answered and told her, "If this isn't an emergency, call me this evening."

"It's an emergency."

"What is it, Bianca?" I stepped into my office but didn't even approach my desk as I waited for her to enlighten me.

"It's Mom."

My heart sunk, and I grabbed the doorknob to brace myself for anything else she had to say.

"She's in the hospital. You need to get here. Now."

"Send me the name of the hospital. I'm on my way." I hung up the phone and turned from my office. "Coco, I'm leaving. If Brian needs anything, do what you need to do and call me only if necessary."

The long strides needed to carry me from the office to my car felt weighted. The thump that hardly went noticed in my chest was pulsating the tips of my fingers. It vibrated my eardrums and had the sides of my face aching. My mom was a healthy woman. I couldn't remember the last time she was in the hospital for anything. Other than her routine check-ups, she didn't mention doctors' appointments often.

But I knew as my parents grew older, that could change.

I started the engine of my car and looked at the name of the hospital Bianca texted. *At least I'm a few miles away.*

When I arrived at the hospital, I ran through the doors. My suit jacket feeling like a barrier between me and where I needed to be. I reached the elevator and called Bianca. "Where is she? I'm at the entrance."

"Third floor."

I looked at the directory. The third floor was the cardiac care unit. *Cardiac care.* I punched my finger on the elevator a few times before the doors opened. As I ascended, my heart felt like it would need an evaluation by the time I arrived. "Bianca," I said when I exited the elevator.

"She's in here," she said as she led the way.

"What happened?"

She didn't respond. Instead, I walked into the room. My mom laid in the bed, her eyes closed. My dad and brother seated around the bed. "What happened?" I asked again.

"She had chest pains this morning," my dad started. His eyes were distant as he spoke. "When she tried to describe them, it was like she was out of breath. I rushed her here." His head fell and he rubbed a hand across his face. "They've run tests and confirmed she had a heart attack."

The thumping in my chest, the throbbing in the tips of my fingers, nothing was moving anymore. I felt like I was under water and anything else said in the room drowned out. The only sound I could hear was the rhythm of the machines connected to my mom. "And now?" I cleared the lump from my throat.

"They are monitoring her. For the next few days," my dad's voice sounded muffled as he spoke.

Mama started stirring in the bed, and Davion jumped from his seat. "Mama, don't move too much." Bianca was in the corner, her head in her hands rocking.

"Deshaun." She reached for my hand, and I let her grab it. "You came."

Everyone's eyes were on me as she continued.

"I'm so happy you are here." Her smile was faint.

"Of course, I'm here, Mama." Her fingers felt soft, delicate as she stroked them over the back of my hand. "I'm going to make sure you have the best available care." I looked over at Davion and asked, "Where are the doctors?"

"They already came in." His forehead wrinkled. "What are you going to do?"

"Whatever I can," I announced before patting my mom's hand and walking out the room. My legs felt like liquid, and I didn't make it further than her door. I leaned against the wall as my fists balled beside me.

"Son," my father's voice was piercing. "She's getting adequate care. I don't know what else you'd be able to do. The best you can do right now is be here for her."

"That answer may be good enough for you, but it's not for me." I pointed toward the room. "That's my mama." I looked toward the nurse's station. "I won't be satisfied until I know for sure she has the best doctors." I walked to the nurse's station. "Who is helping Mrs. Green? Can I speak to her team?"

The woman swept a hair behind her ear. "Sir?"

"I want to speak to her team." An arm rested on my shoulder. "Now."

"Sir, her doctor is doing rounds. They've already been in to speak to her. And will likely return this evening."

"Not good enough," I barked.

"Son." I felt a tug on my elbow. "Come on." He pulled me into his chest like I was still a kid, small enough to carry around. "Let's go. Come sit with her."

I followed him back into the room. "We are supposed to sit here and wait?" I raised my hand before putting it on my hip.

"Deshaun." My mom's voice was a little firmer. "I trust God is in control." Her words were confident. Not anything like I was feeling now. "Have a seat." I sat near the bed and watched her. "Now if the three of you were in church, I'd ask you to pray," she snickered. "But we all know those prayers may hit God's voicemail."

"Mama," Bianca pleaded, "don't joke right now."

"It's true. When was the last time you went to church?" Her eyes were set on me. "When is the last time you prayed?"

"If that's what's needed, I'll pray." I clutched my eyes closed but as hard as I tried, I couldn't find the words. Couldn't find the words to address God. To petition him to help my mom in her situation. I started with, "Dear God," but that didn't feel urgent enough. "Lord, help us." That felt better, but after that it felt like I didn't know what I needed His help with. Finally, my eyes sprang open, and I said, "Can you lead us in prayer, Dad?"

"Oh boy," he said. "That bad, huh?" He half laughed before standing and telling us, "Let's gather around your mama." We did as he asked, grabbed each other's hands, and I bowed my head.

"God, thank you for letting Jocelyn be with us right now." He sighed, "We all know this could have been a different outcome, but God, we thank you." He continued and the more he prayed the more I took note of his words. Of his sentiment. When he finished I felt lighter. "Amen."

"Amen." I wiped the tears from my face. The tears I didn't realize had fallen.

"Awe, bro." Bianca placed a hand on my back. "It's going to be alright. We have to trust it will be."

"Of course, it will be," Mama said. "I need to see one of you get down the aisle. I need to spoil some grandbabies. And," she hesitated, "to retire with my honey." My dad was rubbing her hair back as she continued. "When I'm out of here, at least one of those things we can start seriously talking about. I know it's time for us to retire. This morning was the wakeup call I didn't want."

It was a reality check I could have done without.

THIRTEEN

Leah

The first day at Brown Brothers was better than I imagined. Listening to colleagues talk about the clients and the projects they were working on was the type of thrill I missed. I was taking it all in. The creative director pitching different ideas for a major campaign to the team. The team responding with ideas of their own. It was like I was a spectator of a sport I admired for years.

"I want you to take a look at this project." It was the end of the day, and I was packing up to leave the office. But the creative director was standing near my cubicle with a pointed look in her eyes. "It's a client we won from Bryer." She pointed to my screen and directed me to a file. "The creative works but let me know what notes you have on it." She insisted, "By tomorrow morning, if you don't mind."

My shoulders slumped. I wasn't expecting to stay late on

my first day back to the office. Still, I told her, "Of course. I'll have my notes to you by tomorrow morning."

She tapped on my desk and said, "Thanks," before walking away.

The brief and creative files were open on my screen. I had a full page of written notes when I heard someone clear their throat over my shoulder. Mr. Brown had a hesitant look in his eyes. I adjusted in my seat to face him. "Hi, Mr. Brown."

"Leah." He stroked his beard. "Call me Jacob. How's the first day going?" At first, he was outside of my cubicle, then as he asked he stepped inside, leaning against the desk beside my seat. "Hope you were able to get acquainted." Then his tongue licked out across his lips.

My eyes narrowed. *Did he lick his lips?*

"Yes." I pointed to my screen, turning from him. "Denise gave me this project to review and provide feedback."

I didn't hear him when he moved from his place against the desk. But I felt his breath on the back of my neck when he started speaking. My hand hovered over the mouse as I tried to click around. "I'm sure you'll provide adequate feedback." He lingered on *feedback,* and I wanted more than anything for him to move as far away from me as possible.

The cubicles that surrounded me were all empty. I heard someone a few rows over, but their movements were faint. I didn't suspect Mr. Brown would try anything, but it didn't stop the sweat from forming on my forehead.

I announced, "But I have enough notes for now." I closed the files, picked up the notepad, and searched for my bag. Still, Mr. Brown didn't move.

"Of course." He gave me room to stand from my seat. "Headed out anywhere?"

The limited space between us felt suffocating. With the four walls of the cubicle feeling closer than ever, I said, "Home."

He moved out of my way. Both hands in his pockets as I tried to pass. "Oh, hey." He was walking beside me. "Tell me, why did you end up here instead of Bryer? I heard Bryer offered you a position."

"I thought a fresh start would be better for me."

He tilted his head to the side. "I was thinking it was that you liked me better than Deshaun."

The glass door was in front of me. The only thing between me and the elevators. I watched as they opened, and someone stepped off. They disappeared down a hall. "I hope," I offered, "Brown Brothers will give me the opportunity to grow my talents."

Mr. Brown opened the glass door and watched me step through. "There is growth opportunity here for sure."

His laughter echoed around the small lobby area as I poked my finger against the elevator button. "Have a good night, Mr. Brown." I waved before stepping onto the elevators and leaning against the cold wall.

Kerry and I hadn't spoken since that dreadful day at Bryer. But as I left the building, I decided it was time for us to catch up. I searched my phone for her number.

"Leah?" Her voice was a whisper when she answered. "Is that you?"

I laughed before responding. "It is. Are you okay?"

"Yeah." She groaned. "A late night at the office."

Then I heard the voices in the background. If I listened hard enough, I could recognize some of them. "So sorry." I apologized before saying, "Do you have a minute?"

"For you," she snickered, "anytime."

"I'll be quick. Did you ever have any *strange* encounters with Mr. Brown?"

She repeated, "Mr. Brown?" Then she gasped. "Oh, Jacob?"

I was staring at a wall of the parking garage before locking my doors and looking over my shoulder. "Yes, Jacob."

"Wish you called me before taking the job with Brown Brothers." She sighed. "I would have told you to reconsider."

"Is it that bad? Is he that bad?"

"I would never stay in the office late with him. If others are leaving, I'd leave too. I never had any personal interactions with him, but the way he looked at me. Stories I'd heard about him. It was nothing I'd want to encounter."

My skin began to crawl thinking about what she was saying. I wiped the back of my neck as his words felt like they were still tracing a line along my hairline.

"I bet." I explained, "I was in the office with him and got real uncomfortable. Thanks for letting me know." Before I hung up, I said, "How are things with Bryer. With Mr. Green?"

"Not as good as before." The voices in the background were quiet. "We are losing clients left and right."

I sucked my teeth. "Sorry to hear that."

"Hey, keep a spot warm for me over there just in case."

"I got you," I told her. "Call me anytime, Kerry."

"Thanks, Leah."

As soon as we were off the phone, I pulled out of my parking spot and drove across town to my parents' house. I heard, "Leah, come tell us about your day," before I took a few steps into the house.

Even my dad had a grin on his face as I approached them. "How'd it go?" he asked.

"It felt good to be back in the office." I tapped my laptop bag. "Had to bring a little work home. But I'm thankful to have work that'll make me more money."

My dad laughed. "Got that right." He looked down his nose, over his glasses, when he asked, "Think you'll be leaving us soon?"

Mama tapped his shoulder. "Don't mind your daddy. There's no rush. We know you'll need time to save up and move out."

I nodded. "Unfortunately."

"There's a reason you're here, Leah. Trust that God's plans are better than your own." She stared at my dad. "Right, Lamont?"

He was staring at his half-eaten slice of cake.

"As soon as I can restore my bank account, Daddy, I'll find a place to move."

"I'm believing it'll take no time before everything you lost is restored, plus interest." Mama winked at me, and I hoped, prayed, that she was right.

FOURTEEN

Deshaun

Margot's announcement caught me off guard. I was ready to pop a bottle of champagne, instead I was standing there with my mouth open. The entire room got quiet. "We lost?" I asked. "How did we lose?" The client would be Bryer's largest. It was a win we needed.

"We'll know more after our full debrief," Margot offered as I eyed her.

A full debrief. Like the others stacked on my desk. "Debriefs are only good if we are not repeating the mistakes. Why bother if the results are the same?" I crossed my arms across my chest and widened my stance. "Who won?"

Her hands were wringing on the desk in front of her. "Brown Brothers."

I adjusted the tie around my neck and bent my head side

to side. "Brown Brothers?" I leaned my hands against the table and told them, "We'll connect on the other agenda items at a later time." When nobody moved, I slapped my hand against the table. "You're dismissed."

The room emptied. But Coco was still seated.

"Coco, what is it?" I asked.

"You dismissed a meeting, and we weren't even halfway through the agenda." She was tapping on her tablet. "And rescheduling will be near impossible. You're booked solid for the rest of the week."

"You'll find time, I'm sure." Although time wasn't something I had the pleasure of having. Between Bryer and the other agencies, I was stretched thin. With my mama out of the hospital, I was working with my family on a plan for my parents to retire. Joining the family business felt impossible. Especially with the recent loss of Bryer's client. There was no way I'd be able to turn it over to anyone else.

Coco's arms were now crossed over her chest. Her eyes laser focused on me. She wasn't budging even though I was moving toward the door. "Mr. Green, you're angry because Jacob won the client. Big deal. We keep pushing forward. The creative team is back but likely needs time to get up to speed."

"Get up to speed?" I repeated. Turning from the door, I said, "At the rate we are going, Bryer will be shuttering its doors." I huffed. "It's in their best interest to figure something out. And quick." She tapped something into her tablet, and I said, "Is there anything else, Coco?"

Her hands raised in defense. "I guess not."

"Good, clear my next two meetings. There's somewhere I need to go."

To my back, she shouted, "Where?"

I didn't afford her a response. I continued out of the Bryer offices. Across town to one I'd visited a few times, but not as often. When Brown Brothers opened their doors, I was there. A few times since then, but not since I returned to Greensboro. It was time for me to visit again.

The ten-story building towered over the others nearby. There was limited parking, but I found a spot and made my way through the front doors. Brown Brothers had three floors of the building. The only one I needed was the tenth floor where Jacob sat.

"Good afternoon, Mr. Green," the receptionist greeted me with a wide smile and blinking eyes. "Here for Mr. Brown?"

"Yes," I told her as she started to lift her phone to ear.

"He's getting out of a meeting. Go on in, and I'll let him know you are coming."

I walked toward the glass door and walked down the extended hallway. It mirrored the Bryer offices, with cubicles lining both sides of the space. For a creative agency, it lacked in artistry. The dark wood and modern furniture lacked the creativity I'd expect to see there. None of the faces I passed looked familiar, not until I saw Leah with her head down.

I thought seeing her, after she turned down my offer, would have angered me. It didn't. In fact, my lips lifted. My steps even slowed like she drew me to her. My mouth parted as I neared, but I held in my greeting. I continued to Jacob's office. That's what I was there for. *Right?*

The door to his office was open, but Jacob wasn't inside. The office was as large as half the floor. The bookcases lined with awards and leatherbound books fit him. Jacob was the type to drive around town with a driver. Not because he needed one, but to let people know he had it like that. It was always go big or go home with him. His office was no different. The floor-to-ceiling windows were something he talked about before my return. He bragged about the views of the city.

At the time, his views didn't compare to those of my New York City skyline views. They were better than the views I had at Bryer though. The windows of my third-floor office only had a view of the street, and the coffee shop beside it.

"Jr., what do I owe this pleasure?" My lip curled up. Nobody in business called me that. He only got away with it because we grew up together. But he knew it got under my skin, and he laughed as I faced him. "Still don't like that, huh?"

"You know that." I moved away from his windows.

"Because you'll build your own legacy. Yada, yada, yada." He waved his hand in the air. "Anyway, what are you doing here?" The thought of me building my own legacy wasn't as important as it once was. Not after my mom's heart attack. I didn't tell him that though. Outside of my family, I didn't share that news with anyone. Not even someone I would have considered my closest friend.

I squared my shoulders and outstretched my hand to him. "Congratulations." He took my hand into a firm grip. "Didn't think you'd be able to snatch another client from us." I pulled my hand from his and put it in my pocket. I smirked. "Didn't think you'd be able to do it."

"What is that now?" His head rocked side to side. "The fourth. Fifth?"

"I wasn't keeping count," I said. "But since you are a betting man you might want to take those odds to the casino." My eyes narrowed.

His head jerked back, and laughter fell from his mouth. He

was the only one laughing though. I saw nothing funny about Bryer losing to Brown Brothers on multiple occasions. "Greensboro might not be the city for you after all."

When he calmed, I said, "I can assure you won't win too many more against us."

"As long as the odds are in my favor, I'm not sure I'd bet on that." He pointed toward me. "Was there something else you drove across town for?"

I walked toward his door. "Only to congratulate you in person. Despite the loss, I look forward to going toe-to-toe with you again."

He settled behind his desk and stared up at me. "Me too, Jr., me too."

My hand reached out for the doorknob when I heard him speak again.

"By the way, Leah is proving to be a wonderful addition to my team." I felt there was some extra emphasis added to *my team.* But I looked over my shoulder and saw a familiar face. It was a face that would taunt me as a kid. Convince me to do something I knew very well I shouldn't be doing. Like jumping from the top of the stairs to see how well I landed. Unlike when I was a kid though, I wasn't falling for his bait.

I replied, "Glad it worked out for her." Although glad was the last word that would ever describe my thoughts about him having her on his team.

He stood from his desk again. His eyes narrowed before he asked, "You sure about that?"

I reached for the door again before I said, "No reason not to be." I opened the door and left his office. I was ready to leave the Brown Brothers office, back to my side of the city.

Then Leah stepped out of her cubicle, into the hallway in front of me. Our eyes connected, and she waved. "Mr. Green?" She looked over my shoulder.

"Ms. Moore. How are you?" The angst that built up speaking to Jacob was draining, and I felt the frown leaving my face.

"Couldn't be better."

She was wearing a royal blue shirt and a khaki-colored skirt. My eyes even landed on her shoes. Those were royal blue too.

"And you?"

My voice sounded much raspier as I said, "I'm good. Congrats on the new client." It felt like the next best thing I could say.

"Oh." She wagged her head. "Not sure I had much to do with that. But I am glad for a new client. The campaign is one I'm excited to work on."

"Right." My lips grew tight.

"I should get to this meeting." She pointed over my shoulder. "It starts soon."

"Ms. Moore," I said before she walked away, "I'd like to take you out to dinner again."

She looked around us. To the cubicles, and the people who filled them. Then her eyes met mine again. "I'll consider it."

There was hope in her words, and her response pleased me. "Friday?" I chanced. The ask came out of the blue. Not something I even had time for. For the first time that day though, I felt more optimistic about life.

She started walking past me, then turned and said, "Sure."

My back elongated and my head peered over all the cubicles as I walked out of the Brown Brothers offices. It was like I'd won all the clients in Greensboro as I drove across the city to the Bryer offices. The looming feeling of failure had disappeared. For some reason, a date with Leah was all it took.

I met, "Good afternoon, Mr. Green," from the receptionist with a smile. The art pieces on the wall of the Bryer offices didn't seem as abstract. It wasn't until I saw Coco standing in front of my door that the doom and gloom returned.

"Coco," I uttered. I watched the shape of her eyes, the curve of her lips as I told her, "Mr. Brown sends his greetings." It was slight, but her eyes twitched, and her lips parted.

"You saw Mr. Brown?" she asked.

"I did. Passing along a well-deserved congratulations." I continued into my office.

"How kind. How'd that go?"

"He's confident. Thinks he'll be able to win more of the projects. I'll be sure that doesn't happen." When I was in New York, I don't remember Jacob having such a successful winning streak. I was ready to break it, whatever it took.

"Right." Coco's eyebrows stitched together. She pulled her tablet in front of her face, hiding the rest of her expression. "Is the rest of your afternoon intact?"

"Yes, it is." I sat in my seat and looked at my computer screen. "I need you to clear my Friday afternoon though." I wagged my head. "And tell Jeremy to be waiting."

"Jeremy?" Her tablet moved to her side, and she groaned. "Guess I need to cancel my plans for Friday as well."

I didn't move my eyes from my computer screen when I told her, "That's not necessary. I won't be needing you."

"Oh." She sounded more surprised than I expected. "Got

it." She turned to walk out the office but then turned back. "Something I should know about it?"

"No." There was no need to tell Coco about Leah. That was personal, and anything Coco needed to know about me stopped at business. "Close the door behind you."

"Yessir," she said as she walked out.

FIFTEEN

Leah

What was I thinking? Mr. Green? An actual date? Not like the dinner where he was trying to convince me to take the job. Sitting across from him then had a purpose that didn't involve my heart. Even then it felt daunting to watch him devour his meal, sip his drink, and sit all poised across from me.

I shook my head. Mr. Green was also the man who fired me. Turned my life upside down. He was the reason why I only had room for one dress option in my closet. With my new salary I could afford to buy another one. But with my daddy's insistence, I needed to be saving to move into my own place again.

Nothing felt right, but everything felt clear. I rubbed the side of my temples as I looked at the black dress hanging on the back of my door. I was a pinch away from canceling the date.

From telling him I made a mistake, and I didn't want to pursue anything personal. Not with him.

I looked up to the ceiling. *"Now God, if you want to send me an equally attractive man, with money, who wants to wine and dine me, I'll take him."* I laughed and shook my head, thinking about God looking down with a smirk. "I know, unappreciative."

Because I couldn't afford to get my hair and nails done, I was in the bathroom kneeled over the sink painting my nails. The bright pink made me feel confident and cheerful. If only I could maintain that attitude for the night, I'd survive being in Mr. Green's presence. *I guess I should start calling him Deshaun.*

I looked in the mirror and sighed. *I can't believe I'm doing this.*

Fanning my hands in the air, I made my way back to the room to wait for them to dry. I felt the gurgles in my stomach and wished I would have thought twice about skipping lunch. Then it felt like a good idea because I was busy with a project. Now, it felt like the biggest mistake.

I paced the floor in front of my bed, trying to calm my nerves and forget about the hunger pains. I touched the tip of my nail and decided it was dry enough to pull on my dress. The dress fit like a glove, a little tighter than it was the last time I wore it, but still, it was cute. I did a little twirl and amazed myself by how giddy I felt.

When I finished dressing, I looked in the mirror and I felt my heart beating in my chest. I shook my hands a few times before grabbing my purse. As soon as I stepped out of my room, I bumped into my dad in the hallway. "Oh, where are you going?" *I need to find a place ASAP.*

"On a date." I bit the side of my lip.

"You look beautiful. Hope whoever this lucky guy is treats you right tonight."

The words "he will" were on the tip of my tongue but I decided to keep them to myself. He had been decent in our recent encounters, but there were no guarantees. He did fire me after all. "Thanks, Daddy," I said as I made my way to the front door.

Deshaun left out many details of the night. The only thing he told me was to be ready by six. He had my address, so I expected him to be outside at six. And as my clock changed from 5:59, there was a knock at the door.

I creaked the door open to catch a glimpse of his outfit before revealing mine. "Hello?" My face scrunched up.

The older, distinguished, Black man standing on the other side of the door had a tight-lipped look on his face. His eyebrows furrowed as he asked, "Ms. Moore?"

Considering I wasn't the only *Ms. Moore* in the house, I was thinking the man was there for my mother. Deshaun must have been running late. Although he seemed like a person who would be very punctual. "I'm Ms. *Leah* Moore," I offered, gazing at the man.

"I'm here to escort you to Mr. Green."

Escort me to Mr. Green. I was still standing behind the half-opened door staring at the man on the other side.

"I have instructions to take you to the airfield. The flight is leaving in an hour. We should get going."

Everything that came rushing from his mouth sounded urgent, but overwhelming. I looked over my shoulder and shouted, "I'll be back later," before following behind him. He opened the door of an all-black car and waited for me to climb inside.

It didn't feel like a kidnap situation exactly. Still, I pulled my phone from my purse and texted a message to Janine. Just in case.

Leah: I'm on my way to catch a flight.
Janine: What? To where? I thought you were going on a date with Mr. Green?

Her quick response made me laugh and that was the relief I didn't realize I needed. I explained what transpired. From the driver at my front door, to Deshaun's instructions. Typing it out to her still felt unreal. If I weren't traveling in the *back seat* of a car, I would have thought I was going crazy.

Janine: So, what you are telling me is that you are the luckiest woman alive. Got it. Have fun and find out if he has a rich brother who happens to be single.

Again, I laughed. Then I turned my attention to the driver who was navigating traffic like a pro. *Was he a pro?* I didn't think about Deshaun being wealthy. It should have been a clue at the last dinner I had with him. The fact that he *acquired*

Bryer. Not until the driver showed up at my door with details about a spontaneous flight did I realize it.

I looked up into the sky, as the sun began to set. "Except for Deshaun being *that guy,* I guess you got the rest of my prayer request right." I shifted in the seat and watched as the cars disappeared and so did downtown. "Sir, where are we?" The road narrowed and we were nowhere near the airport.

"Ms. Moore, we are going to the executive airport."

That made sense because we weren't headed in the direction of PTI. I cleared my throat as a large gulp traveled down.

"Mr. Green is awaiting you on his jet." The dark of his eyes met mine in the rearview mirror.

"On his jet?" I repeated more to myself than to him. I wrung my hands together as the sweat started to form a thin layer over them. The car felt like it lacked enough air for the both of us to breathe. After gasping, I asked, "Could you let down the window? Please?"

His eyes caught mine in the rearview again. "Ma'am, is everything okay?"

I was fanning my face with one hand and wiping the other down my thigh. I didn't answer because I didn't know how to alert him that I was not okay. Accepting a date looked like Deshaun picking me up. Passing me a bouquet of flowers and driving us to a nearby, local restaurant. Not having a driver pick me up to deliver me to a private jet. For us to fly to who knows where.

"Ma'am." His voice was a little sterner. "Are you okay?"

"Yes. I didn't expect to fly on a private jet tonight." It wasn't something that ever felt like a possibility or even a dream. If I could afford to vacation again, I was content with flying in a basic seat on a commercial flight.

We approached a hanger, at least what I knew was a hanger from what I saw on movies. There was a lone jet, with an open door sitting in the middle.

"The pilot is one of the best. I can assure you'll be in good hands."

That reassurance didn't do what I would expect. "Great," I mumbled.

The gentleman stepped out of the car and opened my door. He offered me his elbow, which I accepted. My feet felt like boulders as I tried to move them. "I appreciate you driving me, sir." I looked to him and managed a calm look on my face.

"Of course." He held my hand until I caught the railing of the steps leading up to the plane.

Deshaun met me halfway and reached for my hand. I grabbed it and walked behind him up the remaining steps. When we made it to the door, my eyes went everywhere. The cockpit, the seats in the plane. Much smaller than any flight I'd ever been on. Also, much nicer.

Finally, my eyes met Deshaun's and his forehead wrinkled. "Hope this is okay."

"I wasn't expecting this."

"Mind if I give you a tour?"

Behind me, the driver was still standing by the SUV. A small smile on his face as he watched me.

"If you are uncomfortable..." Deshaun's hand tightened around mine. "We can hop back in the car and drive somewhere nearby. But this place I'd like to take you is one of my favorites and I bet you'd enjoy it too."

The gurgling in my stomach returned and I hoped he didn't hear it. "Okay." He interlaced our fingers, and a warmth surged through my body. I looked down to our hands, then up to his face to see if he noticed it too.

He headed into the cockpit, and I assumed he didn't feel it. "Jeremy," he said as his back straightened, and my hand fell from his grasp. "This is our guest for the evening. Leah Moore."

The face of the man staring at me looked familiar. I narrowed my eyes. His eyes were the same shape, his mouth similar. Even his skin tone, the same smooth brown. There was only one difference, the guy looking at me was much younger than the one who drove me to the airport. My shoulders eased remembering the older man's words. "Are you..." I tried to catch a glimpse of the older man out the door, but I couldn't see him. I pointed over my shoulder. "Are you related to..." The man never gave me his name.

"Yes." He beamed. "Jason. Jason Smith. That's my dad."

I joked, "Now I'm not sure I can trust what he said about you being one of the best pilots. He may be a little biased."

Both men laughed. Jeremy's smile when he stopped made me want to compare it to his father's. I imagined it'd be similar.

"We can be in the air in fifteen and I'll show you." Jeremy's chest poked out and I admired his confidence.

Deshaun looked between the two of us. "I'll let you know, Jeremy. Leah seems a little uncomfortable."

Somehow, hearing Jeremy speak eased some of my angst. I didn't let either of them know that yet. "Let me show you the rest of the cabin." Deshaun reached for my hand again as he led me down the slim walkway.

Each seat we passed got a number, *one, two, three.* Until we reached the back of the plane. Ten seats. Not the seats on the plane that looked like they were fold-up chairs at the most, but nice, big, leather seats. Comfortable enough for a nap. In the back, there was a well-decorated bathroom. One that looked like it belonged in a house, not a plane.

"And this is the bedroom." Deshaun stood in the doorway as I peeped inside. "So? What do you think? Can we go up?"

"And where exactly are we going if we do?" I was staring at a small bed with all white linens and plush pillows.

"New York."

My eyes bulged. "Oh, okay."

Deshaun's head tilted to the side as he watched my face. "What do you say?"

If I was nervous about the date, anxiety building on the drive, the coursing through my blood seemed to align. But it felt different. It was calming. "I'm trusting Mr. Smith on this one."

We walked from the bedroom to the middle of the plane and Deshaun pointed to a seat. "I promise you are in good hands." He was beaming before he turned to walk toward the cockpit. Outside the window, Mr. Smith still stood by the car. His eyes never leaving the plane.

With a grip on my seatbelt, I checked it a few times. "Ms. Moore," a feminine voice stilled my hands in my lap. "Hi, I'm Naila."

I released my buckle and gave her a gentle wave.

"Do you need anything before takeoff?"

The most I'd had on a flight was a pack of pretzels and a drink. I couldn't think of anything I would need though. "I'm fine."

She disappeared as quietly as she appeared. Deshaun sat across from me and removed his jacket. He hung it on a hanger I didn't notice behind his seat. Unlike me, he clicked his seatbelt and didn't fidget with adjusting it after. "Would you like a glass of wine?" he asked. He looked over his shoulder and raised a finger to the woman.

"It may help to ease my nerves," I admitted as the engine roared to life.

She brought two glasses and set them on the table in front of us.

"We'll be in the air in five. Buckle your seat belts." Jeremy's voice was more formal than it was when we chatted in the cockpit.

With a hand gripping the seat, I shut my eyes. *"God, please protect us on this flight. Keep us secure in the air, when we arrive, and allow us to make it back here, safely. Amen."* Like any other flight, a prayer was necessary. Even more because of the size of the plane.

"A prayer?" Deshaun's brows stitched together. A firm look on his face.

"Yes," I sighed. "Felt appropriate." I laughed.

The plane started rolling out of the hanger, and I felt my shoulders pressed against the leather of the seat. When we ascended, I watched the small airport below grow smaller. The field of green grass surrounding it grew larger. "Do you fly private often?"

The glass of wine was in his hand. He rested it near his mouth before speaking. "Now that I'm in North Carolina, more than I did."

I reached for the glass of wine. Stroking the stem, I asked, "So you aren't from Greensboro?" I didn't know much about Deshaun. Our last dinner wasn't entirely personal, and I regretted not learning more about him.

"I am but haven't lived there in some time. After college I didn't return."

A younger Deshaun, an image of him riding bikes or bouncing a basketball, laughing with friends, was hard to create. A studious student, in the books, always in the library wasn't as difficult.

"Why now?" I asked.

"My parents are hoping to retire soon." His face was somber. Unlike how I'd feel if my parents were able to retire soon. If they could stop working without worrying about a mortgage or putting food on the table. "They hope I can help with the transition."

"That's admirable." My cheeks flushed. But the look on Deshaun's face was still somber.

He sipped the remaining wine from his glass. "I have two siblings who have been working with my parents since college. I suspect that either one of them or both would be able to take over. But," he turned toward the window, "It seems that my parents don't trust them and want me to take over." My mouth opened slightly. "Of course, I have businesses of my own, and taking over theirs means leaving mine." When our eyes met again, the muscles in his face had softened. His eyes were wide as he asked, "What about you?"

My throat creaked, "Me?"

"Are you from Greensboro?"

I shifted in my seat, stretching my legs before crossing my ankles. "I am. Born and raised. Decided to stay after college." Leaving Greensboro was the plan. Then I had an interview with Bryer, and I decided to stay.

"We'll be landing shortly. Be sure to fasten your seatbelt." That announcement came from the other woman on board.

The comfort level I had reached while we cruised through the sky left fast. The lights of the city below and the idea of landing among them had me on edge.

"Time to land already?" My mouth felt dry, but my cup was empty.

"If it helps, I can hold your hand." He held his hand out for me to take, and I did.

SIXTEEN

Deshaun

I should have picked a further destination. The quick flight from North Carolina to New York wasn't long enough. Sitting across from Leah on the flight was much different than sitting across from her at a dinner table. It could have been that we were on an official date, and I wasn't trying to convince her to take a job offer.

What was I convincing her of sitting across from me now?

When it was time to land, I saw her strained neck and her tense jaw. I reached for her hand. Like the first time I grabbed it, there was something warming when I held it.

I could have held it all night.

"Do you have siblings?" I asked as she stared out the window.

"I do." She nodded but her eyes still didn't meet mine.

"I'm hoping it's a sister."

Her eyes flashed to mine and her eyebrows bunched. "No, a brother."

"Ah, someone who would want to fight me for dating his sister?" There had never been a brother or family member who wasn't excited to have me dating their sister. But that was when I was much younger, before a lot of the success came along. I couldn't imagine anyone would be any less excited for me to date their sister still.

"Date?" She gulped.

"This is a date, right?"

Her eyes lifted and after a few blinks, I asked her, "Is there someone back at home who would want to fight me for dating you?"

"Fight for dating me? No." She shook her head. But her eyes stilled. "Fight for hurting me." She wagged her head. "Probably so. My brother." Then she snickered. "My daddy too."

I leaned in closer, gripped her hand a little tighter. "Glad I don't plan on hurting you." That was obvious. I had no intentions of hurting the woman who sat across from me.

She interrupted my self-declaration when she announced, "Again?"

My eyes narrowed as she shifted in the seat. She stared somewhere behind me as the plane landed on the tarmac.

"Whether intentional or not, I'd count getting fired by you as something hurtful." Her lips formed a thin line.

I grit my teeth. "You're right. Could we leave that part out of our story?"

Her nose scrunched. "It's a significant detail."

It was a significant detail. Something I very much regretted each day. Especially considering Bryer's failings. "You're right." I bit the side of my mouth. "Hopefully they'll understand."

"Liam," she said. "My brother's name is Liam. He's younger, but you can't tell him that."

It reminded me of my relationship with Bianca. Years older than me, and still I treated her like my *little* sister. If anyone hurt her I'd be willing to go toe-to-toe with them. "I can relate." I looked over my shoulder and said, "We should deboard." I stood and grabbed my jacket. Once it was back on I reached for Leah's hand again. It was in mine as we walked toward the cockpit.

Before taking the steps down, she stopped. "Thank you, Jeremy, for getting us here safely." A glimmer in her eyes made me jealous of the attention she was giving him. "I appreciate it."

The black town car was waiting for us near the plane. Instead of the driver opening the door for us, I reached out and waited for Leah to make herself comfortable. I joined her from the other side. The road to the main street was something I'd seen often. I let Leah take in the scenery and adjust to the environment as we rode. "Do you fly all your dates to New York to visit your favorite restaurant?" The city lights had come into view as she spoke.

The skyline of New York was always a comforting sight. One I loved and missed seeing. I turned from it to tell Leah, "It may not seem believable, but you are the first woman, outside of my family, who has been on my plane. I don't hop on flights often for *dates*." I shook my head. "When I fly for business, Coco is always on the plane."

"Coco?" Her hand went to her neck.

"My assistant." Her face turned from mine. "The longer we work together the more she feels like a little sister." I didn't think anything of mentioning Coco, but there was a silence that stung the air after.

As we turned into the thick of New York City traffic, she asked, "So, your other dates. They aren't hopping flights. You stay local then?"

The way she dropped the question made me laugh. I leaned forward and waited for her eyes to look my way. "I've been hyper-focused on my business for years." It wasn't something I was as proud about. The fact that I couldn't balance my business and a personal life. The sacrifice though, it was worth it. "When was your last relationship?"

"Years ago."

The little piece of information comforted me. It did make me wonder what a woman as gorgeous as her, with a gentle personality and ambition, was doing single. "Why?" I blurted.

Her hands were in her lap. Her fingers twisting together. "Guess I've been hyper-focused on my career too. I had a goal, and there hasn't been a man to come along and hold my attention long enough to focus on him."

"Wow." The reality that I could not hold her attention was a wakeup call. Something I didn't calculate in the grand scheme of things. I only considered the fact that I didn't have enough time. Not once did her not having time for me cross my mind. Not making time for us to get to know each other. I tilted my head to the side. "So, if by the end of the night you find me not that intriguing, I'll lose your focus?"

She hunched her shoulders. "It seems a little harsh when said like that."

Both of us laughed. The car was nearing the restaurant, and I told her, "I hope this meal will help my cause. Put a check in the pro column." I pointed. "This is the best Italian food you'll have outside of Italy."

She leaned her head forward and crooked her neck to gaze out the window. "I wouldn't know considering Italy isn't a place I frequent."

"Right. Of course." I looked between her and the restaurant. "Guess you'll have to trust me."

Her hand brushed against my arm and eased whatever the feeling was that had started in the pit of my stomach. I opened the door and stepped out. I reached for her hand, and she followed me.

Before I could leave the car behind she was tugging on my arm. "Are we not going to thank the driver?"

I looked over her shoulder and took the steps back to the car to open the door. "Thanks, I'll see you back here in a couple of hours." I looked to her to ensure that was satisfactory.

She leaned into the door herself. "Thank you, sir." She dragged me away from the car and said, "Better."

Inside the little restaurant, the candles were lit, and music played from the live band in the corner. Unfortunately, the small space couldn't accommodate a private seating area. I did manage to reserve a corner table, away from the crowd though. "Reservations for Mr. Green," I told the hostess.

She looked between the two of us and smiled. "Perfect, your table is ready for you."

Leah followed close behind me. When we made it to the table I waited for her to sit before taking my seat across from her. "This restaurant is beautiful." Her eyes weren't on the restaurant though. She had found the beauty outdoors. The one thing that stood out more than my favorite dish. "Is that the Hudson River?"

"Yes," I told her as I watched the lights flicker over the still water. "We couldn't have that in Greensboro either."

"I guess you're right." Her voice was soft, distant.

The server interrupted whatever thoughts Leah was having as she set a bottle of wine between us. She said, "Tonight we have a branzino, and the twenty-four-layer lasagna."

"Give us a moment," I said. The server walked away, and I told Leah, "I'm sure the specials are amazing. My favorite dish is the chicken carbonara." Then I joked, "I can imagine an Italian grandmother in the kitchen putting her heart and soul into it."

With both her hands raised over the table, she said, "With an endorsement like that, how could I refuse?"

The server took our orders, and as the music played in the background I eased into my seat. "When you aren't at work, what are you spending your time doing?"

I felt her feet brush up against mine under the table as she shifted in her seat. "I volunteer at a community center."

It was the most obvious answer she could have given. Volunteering at a community center was something I could imagine her doing. "I could see that."

She snickered. "I'm not sure if that's a good thing or a bad thing."

"If you enjoy it. I'd say it's a good thing for sure. Do you help kids? Do crafts? Tutor?"

Her head shook and a distant look crossed her face. "I'd do

that. If that was an option. It's a community center for the homeless. Many nights I'm serving hot meals."

It wasn't something I'd ever consider doing. Not outside the community service hours I had to perform in high school. My face twisted. "And you do that often?"

"It was better when I was helping kids?" Her arms had crossed over her chest.

I waved my hand out in defense. "No." I shook my head. "It's not any better or worse. Not something I'd consider doing. That's all."

Her finger tugged on her ear as she said, "Can't say I'd see you doing it honestly. You could reconsider though. Volunteers are always needed."

"With you?" I said, "It's possible." The smile on her face was drawing me in. "Would you like to dance?"

She looked around us. Then toward the band. There wasn't anyone in the restaurant dancing.

I stood from my seat and outstretched my hand. "Someone has to be the first."

She took my hand and stood. I walked us toward the band, to an empty space. The slow jazz of the band wouldn't need either of us to be skilled ballroom dancers. It would be the one thing I didn't find confidence in. But a slow sway, side to side, I could do that. I wrapped my hand around her waist and brought her a little closer and swayed to the beat with her. We moved around the space alone, until a few other couples joined us.

"I guess you're right," she whispered in my ear. "I don't even remember the last time I danced."

"Me either," I admitted. "Could have been prom." That

was so long ago, I could hardly remember the details of the night.

Her head pulled back and she stared at my face. "I have a hard time imagining you as a teenager." Her eyes tightened. "How was that?"

"School, sports, and working at the restaurant," I told her. "So, I guess typical." Most of my teen memories involved Jacob. "You know Mr. Brown, Jacob, and I have been friends since we were young." I hoped she didn't know much about him.

Her back muscles tensed beneath my hold. "Outside of marketing, do the two of you have a lot in common?"

As kids, we enjoyed the same sports. Played games together. Competed for the same girls. As adults, our interests didn't seem to align as much. Still, we managed to find commonalities. "Not anymore," I admitted but didn't elaborate on our differences.

Across the room, the server was setting our plates down. I told her, "We should eat while it's hot." I led us to the table and grabbed my fork to dive in. She didn't. Her head bowed and her eyes closed before I could get the bite of chicken I cut into my mouth. Instead of stuffing my mouth, I waited for her eyes to open.

With them on me, she said, "Don't worry, I prayed over yours too."

"Thank you." I waited for her to take her first bite, and as her eyes closed again, mine narrowed.

"Best outside of Italy, you say?" she asked as her eyes re-opened.

I nodded, hoping she found it as enjoyable.

"A little Italian grandma is certainly in the kitchen.

Thinking Italy needs to be on my bucket list now. Seems like something I'd need to confirm for myself."

"You know, I could have Jeremy adjust the flight plans." With a bite of the chicken in my mouth, it was sounding like a solid plan. When she didn't co-sign, I asked, "Another time?"

"Yeah," she said. "Maybe."

SEVENTEEN

Leah

A chauffeured car ride. A private jet. The *best* Italian food I'd ever tasted. I had to reach behind my arm and pinch myself when we boarded the plane again. If I was daydreaming, I needed to wake up. I didn't want to be too caught up in the fantasy. The sharp pain reminded me it was all reality. A humbling experience. Something I'd want anyone to experience in a lifetime. Knowing it was me, with Deshaun, I was beyond grateful.

But could I take him up on his offer of another date?

The question still lingered between us as we made ourselves comfortable in the seats. I watched him buckle his seatbelt, while I fussed with mine a few minutes longer. To ensure the buckle was not coming loose.

Deshaun wasn't a normal guy. He was handsome in an intriguing way. He was abundantly successful. And he was proving to be someone I didn't mind being around. The effort he was putting into our first date was more than anything any other man had ever done for me.

Then again, none of the other guys I dated had a bank account like Deshaun's. So, the effort they put forth was appropriate *for them*. Deshaun could have done what we did on our first date, every night of the week, if he wanted to.

Did it make it any better? Or worse?

I couldn't decide. And I didn't want to get caught up in all that he could do for me. Because he made it clear that success was his goal. A relationship, even if that's what I wanted, didn't quite align to a successful business. In fact, he could determine it was in the way of his successful business at some point.

That reminder came quicker than I expected when he said, "Sorry." I watched him pull his phone from his pocket. "I need to make a couple of phone calls."

It was late, later than a time when I would be making business calls. Or expecting to receive them. It could have been personal. Either way, sitting in front of him staring at his mouth felt awkward. I offered, "I can move to the room while you make them. I can rest my eyes."

The side of his lip quirked up as he watched me stand. "If that turns into a nap, I'll wake you before we land."

In the bedroom, I toed out of my heels. I placed my purse on the small counter. Then I stretched out across the bed, pulling one of the pillows beneath my head.

At first, I stared at the ceiling and replayed the night. Each highlighted detail made my cheeks warm. I couldn't remember the last time I felt that cared for. Or that a man took that much interest in me. The simple feeling of his fingers intertwined with mine even made my heart thud in my chest. I decided to update Janine.

I reached into my purse and pulled out my phone. Because Deshaun was making calls, I assumed I could too. But I didn't. I texted her instead.

Leah: Dinner on the Hudson River.
Leah: Dancing in front of a live jazz band.
Leah: Who am I?

I laughed as I sent the last text message. I waited for the text bubbles to let me know she was replying. I knew she'd be quick with her response. If it were her sending me the same messages, I would have wanted all the details. I would have been blowing up her phone until I got them too.

Instead of a text though, it was her calling. "Girl, what?" she yelled into the phone. "Are you home? I need to come over and hear this in person." I could hear her shuffling in the background like she was on her way.

"No. Still in flight."

The record scratched, the music stopped, the pause on her end made me think maybe I was losing service. Until she asked, "And on the phone with me?" She groaned. "Why?"

"He had to make some phone calls, so I excused myself to the bedroom." I dangled my toes at the end of the bed. I could have pinched myself again. On most flights I took, I hardly had leg room, let alone an entire bed to stretch out in.

Janine squealed, "Bedroom? On the plane. See. I knew you were God's favorite." She laughed.

I teased, "Guess there are some perks to church on Sunday."

"And you know what?" Her voice was serious when she asked, "What time is church this Sunday? How many services do you think it'd take before I ended up on Jesus's premium blessing package?" We both laughed. I kept laughing until my stomach hurt. "Leah, for real. Everything you are describing is exactly what I've always dreamed of for my life. Guess if you have it, so do I, right?"

"Of course," I said before elaborating, "But—"

"Oh God, no. No buts. Tell me you have already accepted his proposal for marriage. Tell me the two of you will be together till death do you part. I'm thinking shopping sprees across the world. Fancy dinners in restaurants where I can hardly pronounce items on the menu. Being introduced to one of his many single and rich friends. I mean, we could even hit the golf course where I'm sure he's a member."

"Janine." I interrupted her rant. "I don't know about all this."

"I do. Leah, do it for me," she pleaded.

"Even before I lost my job, my life of luxury only included a spa day and brunch on Saturday *and* Sunday. It didn't include drivers and spontaneous flights on private jets. I don't want his wealth to crowd my judgment of him."

"He was nice, right? Considerate?"

"To me." I thought about him and the driver. Then the phone calls he had to make before our date was even over. "What if this is temporary? You've seen the movies," I stressed. "Rich guys can be horrible."

"I mean, not everyone is nice to everybody they meet, Leah. Is it realistic to hold him to those standards?"

"The guy for me could be."

She was quiet. And when she spoke again, it sounded like air seeped from her lungs. "How about you stick around for a while and see what he's like. Give him a chance to prove he is or isn't a decent dude."

"You're right," I told her. "I'll give him a chance."

"Now, go find that fine, successful, rich man who hopefully has a single brother. And play footsie with him." She was laughing before she said. "Oh, and tomorrow morning, I'm coming over for more details of your night."

With a wide smile, I agreed. "Deal."

I sat up along the wall, slipped on my shoes, and grabbed my purse. I opened the door and listened for his voice. I could hear him speaking but still, I walked up the aisle. His eyes stayed focused until he saw me, then a small smile crept up on his face. I eased into my seat across from him, making as little noise as possible. Even putting on my seatbelt, I made myself content with only one tug on it.

"One more call," he said as I watched the clouds and dark night passing us by. The phone wasn't to his ear yet when he asked, "Was the room comfortable enough for you?"

"It was." Then I thought about the footsie Janine insisted on and said, "I wanted to be back out here with you."

The way his eyes gleamed and his smile grew, assured me that was the right choice. "In that case, let me hurry so I can appreciate your company."

His phone was at his ear, and I turned my gaze toward the clouds again. Watching as my eyelids grew heavy.

EIGHTEEN

Deshaun

I hardly ever used the *Do Not Disturb* feature on my phone. But a date with Leah felt like the perfect time to test it out. Unfortunately, the feature didn't stop people from contacting everyone else around me.

By the time Leah and I made it to the plane, Jeremy pulled me aside to say, "Folks are looking for you, Mr. Green. Worried you didn't make it to your destination and said it's urgent you return their calls." His eyes left mine and went up the aisle to where Leah walked ahead of me. "Sorry."

"Thanks," I said. "I'll return their calls soon."

Seated across from Leah, the last thing I wanted to do was pull out my phone. Let alone make a phone call. Especially not about business. We were having a good time. The best time I had in a while. I would even dare to say ever. It was the first time that business wasn't the priority, or top of mind. I was able to relax and have an inviting conversation with someone who was beyond beautiful. Learning more about her felt like it did when I was learning about marketing. I wanted to know everything about it. I read all the books, watched all the videos, studied everything there was to know about it.

Except with her, the only reference I had was her. So, I dialed in. Hanging on every clue she gave me about her life.

Telling her I had to make a few phone calls made my fists clench. Then when she left me alone to go to the bedroom, I appreciated her for not wanting to be in my business. Except, unlike everyone else I would have dismissed from my space, I didn't want to miss her presence.

To say I was a little agitated by the time Davion answered would have been putting it lightly. "Man, I don't ever remember a time when you didn't answer the phone and not call back within an hour. You good, bro?"

It was the pleasantries I didn't need. "What do you need, Davion?"

"Alright." He hesitated before telling me. "It's Dad, he told me tonight he's worried Mama isn't ready to go back even when the doctor releases her."

I eased my fist and told him, "So she stays home." It felt like a simple answer to me.

"Except, the chefs depend on her."

I rubbed a hand across my forehead. If the chefs needed her, there wasn't even anything I could do. I suggested, "It's time for her to start annotating what she does on the daily. It'll be the only way she can transition."

"Okay," he said like the idea was foreign. "Then what?"

"Have her review it with the chefs. Tell them to ask all the questions they have. Don't let them think she'll always be available." I wanted to express the same for myself. Davion couldn't always think I was available to him. But that was a discussion for a day when I had more time. When every word I shared with him didn't mean a minute without Leah in my presence.

"Got it. Thanks." He started to ask something else, and I waited thinking my dad had other concerns. But then he said, "Jeremy mentioned you being with a woman. And not Coco. Are you on a date?" His voice turned whimsical.

It didn't need a response. So, I ended the call.

The door of the bedroom opened, and Leah walked out. I couldn't even move the phone from my face. She had me stalled. Watching her as she approached, I couldn't even hide the obnoxious smile on my face if I wanted to, not even if I tried.

After learning Leah returned to her seat to be near me, the next call I needed to return had to be quick. "Deshaun?" Coco's voice was so low I could hardly hear it over the sound of the engine. "I'm out to dinner, is it important?"

I scoffed. "Is it important? First of all," I started, "you called me. Now I'm returning your call and you are asking if it's important?" I circled my head. "Coco, what'd you need? Jeremy said it was urgent."

She tried to explain, "It was. But I managed to talk to a few managers and resolve it, so..."

"Wait, talked to a few managers, resolved what? What's going on?" Leah's head adjusted to where I could see her eyes. As peaceful as she was, I wanted to watch her sleep. I didn't want to listen to whatever it was Coco needed to tell me. "Forget it, Coco. Enjoy dinner. We'll catch up on Monday."

A long sigh preceded her voice. Much louder than her

earlier whisper when she announced, "Thank you. He can stop eyeing me crazy now." She laughed and hung up the phone before I could offer any other words.

Leah's arm propped on the seat, and her head rested on top of it. Her face was serene. Her chest was hardly moving, it almost looked as if she had stopped breathing.

"We are nearing the executive airfield." Jeremy's voice didn't startle Leah. She didn't even move at the sound of it.

I leaned over the table and tapped her knee, then her hand, but neither woke her. I reached further, to nudge her shoulder, but the plane dipped. My body lunged forward, and my face was inches away as her eyes stretched open.

"Oh, my goodness," she yelped. "Did I fall asleep?" Her hands framed her face. "I didn't mean to fall asleep."

I tried to ease away from her face and into my seat.

Her lips looked to be moving in slow motion as she asked, "Are we landing soon?"

"Yes." My body was aching though. Like it missed the warmth of her skin beneath my fingers. Or the closeness of her breath when I moved in close to her face. "We are." I cleared my throat and watched the lights of the runway come into focus. "You'll be safe in Greensboro, back at home in no time."

Her hands picked at the hem of her dress. "Great."

"Are you okay?" I asked, watching her pick up the dress and drop it again.

"The time you took tonight, the effort you put in." Her eyes never left the hem of her dress. "I appreciate it."

I leaned into her. Listened to each word and watched her downturned eyes.

"What happens when business gets in the way?" She glanced up then turned out the window. "When your ambitions and goals take priority. Is this the right time for you to pursue anything?" Her eyes landed on mine as I contemplated her words.

I straightened my shoulders and leaned back into the seat. The question was valid. Something I should have asked myself. With Bryer, my other agencies, the family business, there was no doubt I had a lot going on.

"Before you, I would say there wasn't room for anything else in my life. Not one more thing." I leaned forward and steepled my hands in front of me. "After tonight, it's important for me to try to find that balance."

"What makes you so confident about me?"

I held her gaze before answering. "For the first time ever, I didn't want to rush home to get in front of my laptop. I wasn't half-listening while trying to plan my next business move." I laughed. "Monday morning meetings are usually something I look forward to over the weekend." I reached across the table between us, palm up. "The entire flight I've been thinking about where I could steal you away to next." I expected her to smile in response and when she didn't, I said, "There must be something about you that has me captivated."

Her hand landed on mine, and she said, "Are you sure?"

"The one thing I've learned through my businesses is that there are no sure deals." I laughed. "I can look at Bryer as an example. But..." I rubbed my thumb across the back of her hand. "I also know that little risk yields little reward. I'm willing to take a big risk right now because what's waiting on the other side would be a big reward." I brought her hand to my lips and placed a kiss across her knuckles. "What do you say?"

Her chest rose and when it fell, she said, "Okay, let's go on a second date."

She raised her finger in the air. "One stipulation though."

"Anything."

"We have to stay in Greensboro." She declared, "It's time you find some local favorites."

"Consider it done." I looked behind me to the cockpit. "I'm sure they are ready to call it a night. We should get out of here."

NINETEEN

Leah

Instead of gardens, or the smell of sweet perfume, the bouquet of flowers made me think of Deshaun. Every day there was a fresh variety on my desk. A handwritten card accompanied it. Leaning down to smell the pink peony, I plucked the card to read the latest note.

Leah, still haven't found a single flower as beautiful as you. – Deshaun

I sat the card beside the others, in a pile forming in the corner of my cubicle. Before starting up my computer, I thought of Deshaun. His smile, although rare, was warm when it appeared. The way his eyes gleamed when he talked about a random fact. How comforting his arms felt when they wrapped around me.

A heavy sigh released as my inbox loaded. I needed to focus on my latest client. Finding a creative for them wasn't coming easy, and I was on a deadline. I clicked through the files reviewing the product descriptions, past campaigns. The upcoming goals for the launch. Nothing was inciting an idea. Not the product, not the company, not even the launch plan.

As a previous client of Bryer, I expected the process to be seamless. I'd worked on their campaigns in the past and had no problem pitching fresh ideas. Unlike Bryer, the team at Brown didn't collaborate. Every person was for themselves, and I missed that aspect of my old team. Our whiteboarding sessions were invaluable.

I hung my head and massaged my temples as I tried to think of possible ideas. Still nothing was coming to me. I read through the client files again, hoping it'd spark something. Scanning over the details, I saw an attached note. At Bryer, we added notes to the files all the time. At Brown, it wasn't something I saw often.

Inside the note were creative pitches. As I weeded through the details, I realized the note was mine. Except the date was months prior. From my time at Bryer. My mouth opened. I scooted away from the computer with wide eyes. I tried to determine how notes from Bryer were in my files at Brown Brothers.

I stood from my desk and grabbed my laptop. I could have been mistaken and needed to confirm what I was seeing. I walked to my teammates and interrupted their typing. "Hey, can you look at this for me?"

Dawn looked up and hunched her shoulder. "Sure."

I placed my laptop in front of her and said, "These notes."

"Okay," she said, nodding her head. "Good ideas." Then

she pointed to me. "How'd you get ideas that quick? Thought you were stuck."

"Look at the date," I told her, pointing to the screen. "Those are from months ago."

"Months ago?" she repeated. "But you haven't been here for months. And..." Her face was twisting as she continued. "This client signed like a week or two ago, right?"

"What about the clients you are working on? Does it have creator notes on it?" I asked.

Kevin replied, "I do." He started clicking around his screen. "These are your notes too."

I leaned over his shoulder to read the file. The client, another one I had at Bryer. "Whose notes?"

"Yours." His voice trailed off. "This is a new client too though. We shouldn't have your notes from Bryer, right?"

I didn't want to accuse anyone at Brown Brothers of doing anything nefarious. I also didn't want to assume it was intentional, or that anyone else even noticed. But having notes from a competing company felt wrong. "I don't think so," I said. "I don't even know how we would have those notes." I rubbed the side of my head as a headache began to form.

Dawn stood and whispered, "Think someone's been using them to get the clients?" Her arms were across her chest. She looked outside of the space we were in. "They wouldn't do that, right?"

The back of my neck began to sweat. My silk blouse would show signs of my nervousness. "Let's not say anything until I have a better understanding of what is going on." I looked between the two of them and waited for each of them to agree. "I need fresh air." I grabbed my laptop. "If anyone is looking for me let them know I stepped outside, please."

I swiped my phone from my desk before walking out. Margot would know if it was normal for the notes from previous clients to travel with their account. I had to call her to find out if that was a thing I wasn't aware of. She wasn't someone I was calling often. But was thankful when she answered after a couple of rings.

Her voice was extra chipper as she said, "Leah?" Laughing, she asked, "Is that you?"

"It is." I gave her a two-minute rundown of my life since the last time we spoke, then asked, "Do you have a minute? I was calling to ask a business question."

"We shouldn't be discussing our clients, Leah." Her voice was no longer chipper, and even a little harsh. She sounded like a chastising mother reminding me to keep my grubby hands off the glass table.

I paced the front of the building. The heat not assisting with my sweat lined shirt. I wiped a hand across my forehead. "Okay," I said. "We shouldn't be discussing details of them. But I have a question. I'm not fishing for information that would give us an unfair advantage. I promise."

She huffed. "Not like the tables aren't already leaning in Brown Brothers favor. Go ahead."

"Thanks." But how did I explain we had notes that could give us an *unfair advantage*. "I was reviewing a new client file and it included notes from me. From months ago."

"How?"

"I don't know." The sun's rays shined brighter, and the heat started to feel excruciating. "Are you still there?" I asked when I didn't hear Margot speaking.

"Which client was it, Leah?"

The fact that the notes included in the file were mine, felt like I could be responsible. Like if it was wrong, I'd be the one caught up in the situation.

"Leah," Margot's voice grew a little louder. "Which client?"

"I shouldn't disclose that."

My eyes clenched closed as she pleaded. Somewhat because of her words, somewhat from the bright sun. "Leah, we are bleeding clients. Over here we are thinking it's odd that Brown Brothers seems to be picking them up at a rapid rate. If there is something we should be aware of, then—"

"Let me talk to Mr. Brown." It occurred to me that I should have started with him first. Although he wasn't the most approachable person, I could have gone to him to figure out what happened. "He may not be aware of the notes, and we can resolve what's going on."

Margot sighed heavy into the phone. "Too bad he wouldn't likely return the clients he's won with the notes. But I get it. This is a sticky situation for you. Please let me know what happens. Mr. Green will be relieved to know it's not his team failing."

I plucked at my shirt. I didn't want Deshaun to be further affected by the issue. The situation couldn't get much worse than it was. "Margot, could you not say anything?"

"Don't keep me waiting too long. I'd like to understand what's going on as soon as possible."

Once the call was over I walked back to my desk. I should have spent my time working on the creative for my client. But the only thing I could think about was ways to approach Mr. Brown. Ways to tell him we had notes we shouldn't have had. Then ask him if they used them in the sales process. It sounded like I was accusing him of stealing clients. I couldn't imagine that would go over well with him.

My fingers tapped on the desk as I continued thinking. I looked at his calendar to see when he'd be available. I needed to meet with him as soon as possible. The sooner the better. But as I scrolled through his calendar, he hardly had any time. *Shoot.*

Before I could find a date and time, my phone vibrated. I peered at the screen and a sigh of relief escaped.

"Leah?" Deshaun's deep voice reminded me of the dilemma, and how I asked Margot not to say anything. In hindsight, she wasn't always the most trustworthy person I worked with.

I whispered, "Hello, Deshaun." In the office of Brown Brothers, talking to him always felt like betrayal in some way. With the news of the notes, it felt even worse.

"Would you mind joining me for lunch today?" His voice didn't sound distressed. Not like I expected if he found out his best friend was stealing accounts from him. He sounded much calmer.

Still, I gulped. "Today? For lunch?" I couldn't be worse at trying to hide a secret.

"I know it's out of the blue. I'm hoping you have time to get out today though."

"Today?" I couldn't stop the parroting. Echoing what he was saying back into the phone. But my mind had no room to think of anything other than what he'd want to talk about in person. Of reasons why in the middle of the day, his very busy day, he'd want to meet with me. Of all our dates, none had been in the middle of the day.

Unless he wanted to confront me about the notes in the

files being mine. I could have wrung my shirt over the sink at that point. Sweat was dripping from every pore.

"Too busy?" He sounded cheerful. Not angry at all. I couldn't understand.

My afternoon was clear, the only thing I needed to do was focus on the project. But with all the information lingering over my head, it wasn't going to be productive. I would have preferred talking to Mr. Brown first, but I owed it to Deshaun to fill him in.

"Okay, if you can make it over to this side of town. I'll meet you at the Corner Café in twenty."

For the next fifteen minutes, I thought of all the explanations I had about the notes. But because I had no idea how they got there, I couldn't come up with a logical one. Everything I thought of sounded like a lie. And a terrible one at that. With five minutes to get to the café, I shut down my computer and left the office.

Deshaun was standing inside when I opened the door of the café. He looked misplaced. His hands were in his pockets, and he stood with a wide angle near the door. He hadn't approached the counter like everyone else. If I didn't know him, and like him a little, I would have found it strange.

I approached and teased, "Let me guess, you forgot your order?"

He chuckled as he continued looking forward. "Worse," he said with a look over his shoulder. "I don't have one and I'm trying to decide between the club sandwich and the pastrami."

"The club."

Before walking to the counter, he asked, "One for you?"

I nodded. "Yes, please." As he ordered I watched him. He

didn't appear furious or upset in the least. When he led us to the table, he even reached for my hand.

"How's your day been so far?" He waited for me to sit before he sat across from me.

"Hectic. A little crazy." I suspected he knew that much. But as he continued I was thinking Margot kept her word. "I'm glad for a break to see you though."

"I was thinking the same." His smile was comforting. "And," he looked around, "I'm thinking I could do this more often." He laughed. "I won't even tell you the last time I left the office for lunch." He looked up then back to me and said, "In fact, I'm not sure I'd remember."

I cringed. "I'm glad you stepped out of your comfort zone."

They called his name, and I was glad for a reprieve from the conversation. I closed my eyes. *Dear God, please let me figure out this situation before this causes more harm than good.* I waited for a moment before whispering, "Amen."

"Praying before you even have your food?" He sat a plate in front of me. "That's a first."

I smirked. "Not exactly." I closed my eyes again for grace then told him, "Still not blessing your food before you eat it?"

He lifted a finger in the air then closed his eyes. It wasn't long before his eyes sprang open and he said, "I think that was it." We both laughed.

"How are things going at work?" It slipped from my mouth before I could even think about what I was asking. Work, Bryer, business, it wasn't something I wanted to discuss.

It made it worse when Deshaun said, "Bryer is getting the best of me." My heart felt like it was exploding into pieces of confetti. "I can't seem to figure out why we aren't winning clients." He took a bite of his sandwich and as he chewed, I felt sweat forming a layer on my forehead. "Proves everything in life isn't easy."

If I was in an interrogation room, they would be preparing the cuffs. The way I was sweating and feeling the proverbial heat, I was about to spill everything I knew. I'd indict myself before he finished his last bite. I took a deep breath ready to tell him all I knew when he spoke again.

Wiping his mouth, he said, "I've been thinking."

I was hanging onto his words, hoping mine wouldn't rush from my mouth before he said whatever was on his mind.

"How'd you feel if I went to church with you on Sunday? You said it's an open invitation, right?"

I coughed on the sip of water in my mouth. Patting my chest, I narrowed my eyes. "Church with me on Sunday?"

"Are you okay?"

I nodded. "Yes. Guess I didn't expect you to ask me about church." *Especially when I have something incriminating to say.* "But, of course, church on Sunday. Open invitation. I'd love for you to join me."

"Thank you." He reached across the table and asked, "Could we go together?"

"We can," I told him. What I had to share didn't seem as important anymore. Not in the *grand scheme* of things. After years of not going, Deshaun returning to church felt more important. More important than me ruining his day further. I kept the details to myself, and decided, I'd gather more information then I'd tell him.

TWENTY

Deshaun

The last time I went to church, I'm pretty sure I wore
something my mama picked out. That day, I was rocking my
favorite blue pin-striped suit and slate gray tie. I was staring at
my shoes when Leah's front door opened.

"Hello there?" The door opened wide, and her eyes trailed
from my shoes to my shoulders. "You look nice enough to be in
the pulpit." She turned to lock the door, and I looked down at
my tie.

"Is it too much?"

"No sir." She glanced over her shoulder. "You look
good."

"So do you." The yellow dress she wore defined her curves.
Headed to church, the thoughts it invoked weren't appropriate.
If it were a normal date, I'd let them wander. *Did people do
church dates? Was that a thing?* "Have you ever taken a man to

church with you?" I opened her car door and waited for her to get comfortable inside.

"No." Her answer was definitive. "I have not. And this should be interesting."

"I was thinking the same." I walked to the driver's side and asked her where her church was. After she told me, I asked, "Do you go to the same church as your parents?"

I picked her up at her parents' house a few times but hadn't met them. I wasn't exactly ready for a run in with them yet.

"No. I found this church after I graduated. They still go to my childhood church. It's a little more traditional."

"Versus?" I had only been to one church growing up. My parent's church. The church they still went to every Sunday. It could have been traditional, but I didn't have much to compare it to.

"A little modern. We don't have a set agenda for the service. Aren't singing from a hymnal. Our songs have a little beat to them." She hunched her shoulders. "You'll enjoy it."

Outside of getting encouraging words, I didn't consider the rest. "I hope so," I told her. The closer we got to the church the more panicked I became. When I was a kid, the newcomers had to stand and introduce themselves. I'd been in many rooms with complete strangers for business meetings. But the thought of speaking in front of a church after being outside of it for so long felt daunting.

My mouth grew dry before I asked, "Does your church make visitors stand?"

She shook her head. "No." She laughed and turned toward me. "Would that be a problem?"

I pinched my fingers. "A little."

She rested her hand on my forearm. "Don't worry, all will be well."

Her words were comforting. So much so, I felt I already had my encouragement for the day. But it was too late to back out. The navigation let me know we had arrived. Leah led the way inside. Others walked along with us. People greeted her, she hugged a few necks and shook some hands before she finally found a seat in the middle.

On the other side of Leah was an older woman wearing a huge church hat. It looked like something I saw when I was younger at church with my parents. It even looked like something my mama would wear. The woman leaned into Leah's ear, and concealed by her hat, I couldn't hear what she said. After she pulled away, Leah looked over at me and laughed.

Before I could ask what the woman whispered, the choir in front of us started singing. I bobbed my head and clapped along where appropriate. People around me were standing, belting out the lyrics of the song. Leah was right along with them.

The pews weren't like a boardroom, my office, or a conference room where I was most comfortable. It was odd that I felt at ease. The choir transitioned to a new song, and more than the first, the words of the chorus uplifted me. *"Even when it's not, it's still all well."*

Bryer and all the clients we were losing felt like the *not*. The all well felt hard to appreciate in the moment, but I was trying to get there. Before church that morning, I was feeling like my streak of *luck* in business was coming to a tragic end. It was a blow to my confidence. But as the words of the chorus continued, I knew something would come of the misfortune.

The choir's words ended, and the music rolled to an end.

A man in a tailored suit stood behind the podium. He didn't look like the pastor from my childhood. He was younger and wasn't rocking a pastoral robe. But when he opened his mouth his voice was as distinguished. A voice that quieted everyone listening as he began to speak.

When I was a kid, I would have exited for children's church. If I did sit in on the sermons I'd grow tired five minutes into it. That day I tuned into every word he said. He walked the length of the stage and my eyes followed, back and forth, as he quoted scripture. He offered relatable stories that were familiar to my specific situation. *Had he sat in on one of my client calls? Did he know how Bryer was failing?* It felt like it.

"Oftentimes, we depend on ourselves for the strength we need to get through day to day. Our confidence is so high, that it seems nothing can shake us. But when it does, it's a reminder of where our strength comes from." The pastor stopped pacing and stared out over the crowd. His hand outstretched, with one pointed finger directed at us, he said, "Believe me. It's not from within." He looked up to the dark wood beams of the ceiling. "It's from above. The sooner we allow ourselves to realize it, the less we will struggle with everyday battles."

As he continued I eyed Leah. Her silhouette resigned as she listened. *Had she made a call?* Being at Brown Brothers she knew how many accounts they were winning from us. Could she have put in a special request to the pastor for his sermon that morning? *That's foolish.*

I shook my head and gave my attention to the pastor. He was noting people in the Bible who grew confident in their actions. Who disobeyed God along the way. And the fate they endured because of it.

Being that I was years removed from church, the stories no

longer stood out in my memory. Still, I took heed. I wasn't taking notes like Leah, but I was engaged.

"Is there anyone here who is ready to stop leaning on their self, to give their life to God?" I felt all eyes were on me. I adjusted my tie, pulling at the end of it as I tilted my head downward. I didn't have that strong desire to take that walk. To walk to the front of the church.

Hand claps started around me as a man from the back of the church stood. Then another young woman from the front of the church followed. I released a breath held up in my chest.

Minutes later, they dismissed church, and I stood feeling much lighter than I did walking in.

"You good?" Leah asked from beside me.

"I am." I asked, "Do you usually grab something to eat after church?" I tapped my stomach. "I'm feeling a little hungry."

She laughed. "Trying to extend our time together?"

"Could you blame me?"

"I don't mind grabbing a bite to eat." She raised a finger in the air. "But first let me introduce you to some of the women of the church." She hunched her shoulder. "If not, I'll never hear the end of it."

There were a few women nearby and as Leah introduced me, their eyes lit up. Each of them hugged around my neck, and the small talk and pleasantries didn't even bother me. "It was nice to meet you ladies," I said with a grin and a wave as Leah walked us away from them.

We ended up at a brunch spot she suggested. As we sat across from each other I felt a sense of gratitude swelling in my chest. "You know," I sat my menu to the side, "halfway through that sermon I felt the pastor was talking to me."

She was still looking over her menu when she offered, "That's the beauty of a sermon. It always feels personal."

I felt a rumble of laughter starting in my chest. Before I released it, I said, "Here I was thinking you put in a special request to the pastor. To make sure I felt the message this morning." We both laughed, disturbing the people beside us. I held a fist over my mouth and bent my head. "Crazy, right?" I asked when my laughing subsided.

She side-eyed me and said, "Like there's a hotline." Her head shook from side to side. "And how long has it been since you've been to church?" She wiped a hand beneath her eyes. "Jesus is on the main line is only a song. You know that, right?"

With her still laughing, a grimace came over my face. "Must be too long because some of the Bible stories he shared aren't familiar anymore."

Her arm reached across the small table, and her hand rested on top of mine. "There's no time like the present to change all that. You know?"

I nodded in agreement. "Can't say that I'll be a regular yet. But I did walk out feeling much better than when I went in," I told her, "And that song before he preached." I thought of the words and made no attempt to sing them. "Even when it's not, it's still all well." The tune played in my mind. "Those hit me something serious."

She bit the side of her lip, and something else hit me. Something I chose to ignore considering we were still discussing church. "Hmm," she hummed. "Never knew someone talking about church could be so attractive." She looked away.

On the opposite side of the table, the server cleared her

throat before asking us what we wanted to order. I was somewhere between relieved and disappointed by her distraction.

Leah said, "I'll have the chicken and waffles and an orange juice." After ordering she looked at me, and I told the server I'd have the same.

"Attractive, huh?" Once the server was out of earshot my eyes were tracing the features of Leah's face.

We'd been on several dates, and I enjoyed each of them. Getting to know her was my new pleasure. Any free minute I could find in my day, I wanted to fill with Leah. There weren't many, so I appreciated each of them. Still, I wasn't sure how she felt about me. She seemed to enjoy our time together but hadn't expressed it specifically.

She adjusted in her seat. Her hand went to the side of her neck as she gazed at me. "Very attractive." Then she adjusted again, moving her hand to her lap. "Until now, it's always been a physical attraction. Now." Her sentence became softer, but I listened harder. "It's deeper than that."

"Thank you for the opportunity to get to know me on a," I cleared my throat and shifted my legs, "deeper level."

"By the way," she straightened, "you are welcome to join me any Sunday of the month."

I appreciated the open invitation. "Thanks for that." I admitted, "If things at Bryer don't start to improve, I could use a constant stream of motivation to keep me going."

Her eyes shifted around the room. They landed on the window as my eyes narrowed.

"Is everything okay?" I asked.

Something was bothering her and every nerve in my body was on high alert. Not since the time a kid bullied Davion in school did I have the same feeling. And back then, it was the first and only time I fought someone. I would have done it all again to ensure my brother was safe. Older and wiser, I was confident I wouldn't need to fight someone. But the way my fist clenched, I was starting to question that. "Leah?" I asked again, urging her to tell me what was going on.

"How much do you trust Mr. Brown?" She clarified, "Jacob."

The tension in my jaw didn't relax, and my fists stayed clenched. "I've known him most of my life and call him a friend. I'd say I trust him well." That feeling inside wasn't easing though. Even saying the words out loud, I knew more about Jacob than I'd share with most people. When Leah's face didn't ease, I told her, "I trust him with you."

Her eyes widened, and her mouth opened. "What do you mean?"

The people beside us were close enough to hear our conversation, so I lowered my voice. "He's been known to approach the women on his staff. I trust he wouldn't with you though." Then again, there was nothing that Jacob knew about Leah that would prevent him from doing it. "Has he said anything inappropriate to you?" People didn't know that Leah and I were dating. If Jacob did, he wouldn't approach her, but because he didn't know, he could have. My stomach felt like it was turning inside out.

Leah's eyes narrowed. "No," she said with her lips tight. "He hasn't."

Our server approached with our food. She was in tune with the most inappropriate times to return. As she placed our plates down, my nose flared. I needed to understand what concerns Leah had about Jacob.

"Thank you." Leah's voice was still soft as she looked up at the server.

Her head bowed and mine did too. Before praying, I took a long, deep breath. *"God, give me the strength to handle whatever it is Leah is about to tell me."* I was about to open my eyes when I remembered I had food in front of me. *"Oh, and God, thank you for this food."* I wagged my head. *"Amen."*

Leah was grabbing her fork. "I was about to tell you I prayed for yours too." The corner of her mouth ticked up as her face rose from her plate. "And looka here. God is showing out this morning."

"He sure is."

TWENTY-ONE

Leah

There was a feeling of guilt I couldn't shake. The notes in the client files shouldn't have been there. But when I approached Jacob about it he made it seem like no big deal. He didn't give me the impression that he was in any way concerned. It was questionable, but I also didn't know much about him.

The thought of talking to Deshaun about him churned in my head for days. But I knew that was a delicate area. A thin line I wasn't sure I could cross and recover from. The two were friends, but also competitors. I was dating Deshaun, but I worked for Mr. Brown.

Seated across from Deshaun, with him opening up about church, my feelings grew deeper. And the guilt was coursing through me like a wave. I knew enough about a guilty conscience. It wouldn't subside until I said something or did something that would make the situation right.

A few bites of food at least allowed my stomach to settle. So, when Deshaun circled back to the discussion about Jacob, I didn't feel like I was walking across broken glass.

"There are some things he does in business that I'm not sure I contend with." That was vague enough to resolve *nothing*. I sighed. "This is a hard topic for me to discuss," I admitted.

The wrinkles in Deshaun's forehead smoothed out. His hand that he held in a constant fist since I mentioned Jacob's name, settled flat on the table. "I don't want you to feel you can't discuss work because we are competitors." He lifted his hand in the air, and as it hovered, he said, "If it's easier not to discuss, we can do that too."

The restaurant was clearing. Each table beside us was empty. If I needed to tell him, I had the space and opportunity. Still, I didn't know if it was appropriate. I couldn't find a way to present it to him. I copped out and said, "Let's not."

We finished our food, but before we left Deshaun asked if we could spend more time together. "I have somewhere to go."

His shoulders slumped as he stood. "My bad. I got ahead of myself. I should get you home." He reached for my hand and guided us outside.

"You could come with me."

He opened the passenger door of the car and waited for me to get in before he asked, "Where to?"

I looked at his tailored suit and told him, "We should change clothes first."

He looked down at his suit and back to me before he said, "I can take you home and come back."

"Or we can meet there," I told him. "It may be easier."

Without knowing where *there* was, he agreed. "Sure, we can do that. Send me the address."

After he drove off from the front of my parents' house, I hurried into my bedroom to change clothes. The extended time with Deshaun had me excited to get back to him.

"Leah." I heard a knock as I pulled a shirt over my head. "How was church today?" my mom asked after she opened the door.

"It was a great sermon." Everything about church that day was better than I could imagine. It was the first time I went to church with a guy I was dating. "Deshaun enjoyed the service too." I laughed to myself as I pulled my hair into a ponytail. "He thought I put in a request for the sermon, so it'd speak to him."

Mama's face wrinkled and she laughed too. "A request?" She shook her head. "Must have touched him deep down in his soul." She poked at her belly. "You headed to the community center?"

"Yes," I told her, "and Deshaun is coming with me."

Her eyebrows wriggled. "Oh, okay, looks like things are getting serious."

I hunched my shoulders. "We'll see." I kissed her cheek then said, "I should get going so he isn't confused when he gets there."

On my way to the center, I thought about my last dates with Deshaun. They weren't as elaborate as the first, and still, we had a good time. Between our dates, when we talked on the phone, I felt like I did with my first boyfriend—extra giddy.

Those feelings flashed back as I pulled my car into a parking spot next to his. He had the phone to his ear and was facing the building, but as I got out he turned my way. A smile flashed across his face, and he ended his call. "The community center?" He opened his arms and I walked into them. "Wasn't expecting this." His tone was skeptical.

"Not up for it?" I craned my neck to look at him as I pulled out of his embrace. "I'll understand if you don't want to join me."

"Oh." He wrapped his fingers around mine. "I'll join you. Didn't know what to expect when you asked me to meet you." We walked, hand-in-hand, to the entrance.

Inside I told him, "This is the center." We walked through the dining room. "Here's where we will serve." I pointed down the hall. "And on that side is where the members who are fortunate to have a space for the night will sleep." I guided us toward the kitchen. "And this is the kitchen."

Looking over her shoulder while she stirred a pot, Ms. Carol said, "Hey, Leah." She looked to Deshaun. "Oh, and who is this?"

Excited to introduce the two, I said, "This is my friend, Deshaun." I looked between the two of them.

Ms. Carol had her eyes set on him. "Okay, Deshaun." She wiped a hand across her apron before reaching for his. "Ready to help?"

Deshaun wiped the back of his neck before responding, "I can't promise I'm the best cook. But sure."

She nudged his side before saying, "Don't worry. Not much goes on in this kitchen without my guidance."

The other volunteers confirmed with grumbles and laughter.

Ms. Carol eyed me before waving a hand in my direction. "Leah, don't worry about him. He's safe right here." She winked.

"Great, I'll make sure the tables are set," I announced before leaving the kitchen. I headed to Liam's office though. I would have to tell him about Deshaun before they bumped into each other. Before Liam felt the need to wear his *big brother* shield.

I didn't expect to see Liam behind his desk with his head hanging low. "Hey, you okay?" I said as my eyes narrowed.

With a heavy sigh, he shook his head. "Wish we had more beds."

The demand always outpaced the availability. "I'm praying that one day that won't be an issue."

"God will hear us soon enough." He scribbled something on the notepad in front of him.

"By the way, I brought in an extra set of hands."

His head raised and the smile on his face was telling. "Oh yeah?" It widened as he asked, "Janine?"

I put a hand to my hip and chastised him. "Sir, what happened to Michelle?"

He laughed. "She's still around. But you know in case that doesn't work out." He lowered his voice, "You know I've always had my eyes on Janine."

My eyes rolled. Janine and I had been friends for longer than I could remember. And Liam had been chasing her from the beginning. She'd always laugh it off, and I knew he didn't have a chance with her. "Better put all your energy into Michelle." I smirked. "It's a different *friend*." Deshaun and I hadn't discussed anything more than that. Sure, we were dating, but the topic of more didn't come up. I had my thoughts on the situation, but wanted to see if we were on the same page.

"A *different* friend." Liam stood from his seat and craned

his neck like Deshaun would appear out of thin air. "Where? A guy friend? Who is it?" His chest poked out a little further. "You brought a *boyfriend* up in here?"

I tilted my head to the side. "Relax. He isn't a boyfriend." I shrugged my shoulder. "Yet."

Liam grumbled as he shook his shoulders. "I'll be out to meet this *not a boyfriend* when I wrap up this paperwork."

"And Liam, when you do, be cool. Okay?" I turned to walk out and heard him grumbling more.

The dining room was in disarray when I entered. There weren't any other volunteers around. I had to move all the tables and chairs where they needed to be for dinner. There were a few random boxes on the floor and I carried those to a corner. I was shaking off my hands when I heard, "Green beans," behind me.

Deshaun was standing with the pan in his hands, an apron over his clothes, and a questioning look. "Where do they go?" He looked at the tables I arranged then said, "Is this space big enough for everyone who will be eating?"

I wagged my head. "More or less. They make it work." I pointed to the serving table. "We can place those right there. We put all the food here buffet style. They'll form a line, and we'll serve them." I plucked the plastic apron and said, "Looks good on you."

He chuckled then looked over his shoulder. "Ms. Carol insisted I not mess up my clothes in *her* kitchen." His hands went to his pocket. "Guess I didn't know where we'd end up today."

"Next time I tell you we should get changed, I'll make sure I specify further." I swayed side to side. "My casual is more t-shirt and leggings." I looked at his cashmere sweater and slacks. "Didn't think yours would be sweater and slacks." I laughed.

"Considering I wear a full suit every day, I thought this would be casual." He slid his finger down the side of my face. "It's cool though. I'm sure we'll have more time together for us to figure out those small things."

"Deshaun!"

His head spun around. "Whew, that sounded like my mama for a minute." He laughed.

I followed him to the kitchen where Ms. Carol instructed us to take the remaining dishes out to the dining room. We made a few trips before everything was set and ready for the members to come through the line. Deshaun stood beside me. With a steady hand he scooped green beans onto each person's plate.

The line dwindled and as we were cleaning up, Liam entered the room. He beelined it straight toward me. "So," he looked at Deshaun beside me, "is this your *friend?*"

My chest heaved and I nodded.

Before I could introduce them, Liam's hand outstretched.

"I'm Leah's brother." His chest poked out and his jaw was tense. "Liam." They shook hands and Liam said, "Thanks for joining us today. We are always in need of more volunteers." He gave a glaring stare as his arms went across his chest.

I couldn't remember the last time Liam met a guy I was dating. It could have been in high school, back before Liam could even flex a muscle. Even then he was overprotective.

"It was a pleasure being here." Deshaun was stacking trays from the table as he spoke. "It seems like a worthy cause, and a need for the community."

"Leah," I heard from the kitchen and wanted to ignore Ms. Carol but knew better than that.

"I'll be right back." I eyed Liam as I backed away. Without supervision I didn't want him to go overboard in his *brotherly role*.

Ms. Carol was standing over the pound cake, cutting it into slices. "Deshaun seems to be a decent guy." She didn't look up from the slice she wrapped in a piece of foil. "Seems like someone who could be better than a friend."

"We'll see, Ms. Carol." I sighed. "We'll see."

"If I was a little younger, I'd give you a little competition." She winked.

"How'd your husband feel about that?" I laughed. "I'll take this cake out." I reached for the cake and told her, "You know this is everyone's favorite."

"These are for the two of you." She held up the foiled wrapped slices of cake. "I'll put them over here for you."

"You're the best, Ms. Carol," I said as I exited the kitchen with the cake in hand.

Liam was on one side of the room talking to a member, and Deshaun was standing behind the serving table. "What now?" he asked.

I pointed to the cake. "Now dessert." When I placed it in front of him, his eyes widened.

"Wow. Is that homemade cake?" His mouth was salivating.

"It is," I told him, "Ms. Carol saved a piece for each of us. We can grab it when we finish here." The members made their way through the line again. Each person grabbing a slice of cake before hurrying back to their seats to devour it. "Alright," I told him as I collected the crumbs, "That's it for today."

He followed behind me to the kitchen where we said our

goodbyes to the volunteers. Deshaun lingered a little in front of Ms. Carol as she commended him on his listening skills. "Thanks, Ms. Carol," he said.

She wrapped her arms around his neck and winked at me as their hug delayed.

With the cake in hand, I told him, "Seems like you're popular with the wiser ladies."

"There's only one lady I'm interested in being popular with." He stood in front of my car door. "How is she feeling?"

"Pretty smitten." I laughed. "How'd it go with my brother?"

His eyes widened and he held up a finger. "I should eat a piece of this cake first." After chewing and closing his eyes, he asked, "You sure he's your younger brother?"

"According to birth order. Yes." I bit the side of my mouth as I thought of all the things Liam could have said.

"Well, he wanted to be sure I had good intentions." Deshaun shrugged. "And I can't blame him for that. He was direct and to the point. I respect a man who doesn't waver."

I opened the foil on my cake. I needed a bite too. "What'd you tell him?" I kept my eyes on the lemon glaze.

"Told him I intend to figure out if this can be something long term. Something I didn't see coming." I felt the heat from his body as he moved closer to me. "And in the least, it'll never be my intent to hurt you."

A gasp left my mouth as it opened. His lips crushed into mine, his arm wrapped around my waist. The kiss was anything but *friendly*. When he pulled away I was panting. "Oh," I muttered. It wasn't like the soft, gentle kisses he gave before. It was more needy, passionate, deliberate. I stuffed another piece of cake into my mouth.

"Are you okay with my intentions?"

I chewed the piece of cake until the only thing that remained was the aftertaste of lemon. "Yes." I wiped a hand across my forehead. "I am."

He rubbed a hand down my arm as I felt the chill of the air. "Your brother also told me that they aren't able to serve all the people who need beds each night."

"Unfortunately, not."

"The city should allocate more funds in the budget to make sure that's possible."

I released a long breath. "Sadly, the population seems to outpace the increase each year. Not even the donations they collect can keep up." My arm shivered beneath his touch.

"We should get out of here." He held my door open.

"Thank you again for coming and helping in the kitchen."

He shoved his last piece of cake into his mouth as I settled into the driver's seat of my car. "With Ms. Carol's cake, I may become a regular." He leaned down and kissed my cheek. "Get home safe."

TWENTY-TWO

Deshaun

Leah was a dealmaker. My offer for her to join my family for Thanksgiving didn't seem like a deal though. Not until she countered with a proposition of her own. I would have to join her family, and volunteer at the community center. Spending the day with her, whatever way we spent it, felt like a deal worth compromising for.

At least it started that way.

When we walked into the community center, I expected it to be like the first time I volunteered. A few volunteers, a line of people ready to eat. Not a line of people out the door, and more volunteers than I could count.

Leah led us past the members lined up and ready to eat, as someone shouted, "Hey, the line is back there." We went straight into the overcrowded kitchen.

Ms. Carol appeared from the masses shouting directions.

I approached her and asked, "Ms. Carol, how can I help?"

She looked between me and Leah and said, "Glad you're back, honey." She winked at Leah as if I wouldn't notice, then said, "You remember how you did those green beans last time?"

"Yes," I said with a nod.

"Go ahead and do it again, I'll need four pans." She held up four fingers.

"I got it." I accepted the plastic apron she had outstretched. "I'll be in the corner, if you need me." Leah exited the door as I found a little space to start the green beans.

The woman beside me bumped my elbow. She wasn't to blame though. The limited space with a few volunteers became claustrophobic with more than a dozen.

She huffed, "Sorry." Her arms clutched her sides. "Wouldn't be bad if we had a little more room in here." A frown appeared on her face. "I'm Diane. What's your name?"

"Deshaun." I watched the green beans pour from the bag into the pan.

"Glad you are here." She shared, "You know, I come here every year."

I was in for a story.

"I vowed no matter what, if God helped me out of that situation, I'd do my part to volunteer as often as possible. Always on Thanksgiving."

I didn't have to pry for more details. She expounded as I mixed the seasoning into the green beans. "This place gave me a warm meal and a place to lay my head for twenty-three months. Until I was able to afford a place of my own."

My hand stopped moving, and my eyes flashed to hers. I didn't mean to stare, not in the way I did. She looked well put together—hair done, nails done, bright smile. Even her shoes looked fresh.

She smirked. "He's brought me a mighty long way."

If I had to guess, she wasn't much older than I was. I wondered how long ago it was when she depended on the community center. Still, I didn't want to get too far into her business.

"Ah," she sighed. "Anyway, I'm glad we have all these people here." She banged her fork on the corner of the pan. "Especially Leah and her brother." Her arm flexed as she continued mashing potatoes. "Those two right there are amazing humans."

I felt my chest swell as she complimented Leah. I couldn't agree more. Leah was an amazing human being. Being around her made me feel like a better person.

A silence fell over our corner of the kitchen as everyone focused on Ms. Carol's orders. "Less talking, more cooking," she shouted at one point.

I finished my four pans of green beans, and Diane's pans of mashed potatoes were done too. Ms. Carol directed me to butter the rolls and I appreciated the simple task.

Diane joked, "You must not cook often, Deshaun." She pointed at my hand is it glided over the roll, leaving a trail of butter in the path.

"Not as much as I should considering my family has operated restaurants my whole life." I shook my head. "One would think I would have picked up a little skill by now."

Diane laughed. "One thing I've learned, there's no time like the present to make a change." She had a crooked smile when she said, "And this is a start." Diane didn't know much about me, but much like Leah, her kindness extended toward me effortlessly. I was starting to think it was something about the people in the community center. They cared more about those around them than most other people I encountered.

"You have a point," I said. My parents and their pending retirement plans came to mind. It wasn't like I'd need to cook in any of the restaurants to run the business. But knowing more about the food operations would be a plus. *Was I considering the possibility of the family business?* I shook my head and buttered the last of the rolls.

I was ready to take on another task when Ms. Carol let us know it was time to start moving the food. She told us to take out a single pan of each dish. I walked out of the kitchen with green beans in one hand and rolls in the other.

The dining room was nothing like it was the first time. Fall colors abound, along with plants and décor on each of the tables. I smiled over at Leah as she placed a centerpiece. "This looks amazing," I told her as I approached.

"It is." She had a somber look on her face. "For some of these people it'll be the nicest thing they've seen since the holidays last year."

I rubbed a hand across my chin. I couldn't even count the number of fancy dinners I'd been on in the past couple of months. Let alone since the holidays last year.

"I'm glad I came," I said. The small room and the number of people that would soon feel it was a reality check. If I wasn't there, I would have been home sitting on the couch watching TV. I wasn't ashamed of where I was in life. But the day was reminding me that I could be doing more in the community, with my family.

She stood on her tippy toes and placed a gentle kiss on my lips. "Thanks for being here."

After we parted, my tongue licked across my lips, and I wished the kiss could have lasted longer.

But it was time to serve. Members shuffled into the room. Every available seat filled, and every corner of the room stood a person who couldn't find a chair. We went through pans and pans of food. Standing in the line serving each person, one by one.

After serving the last person, Leah said, "That's it."

I looked around at all the dishes and decorations. "Do we start cleaning up now?"

Leah assured me, "Another set of volunteers will come in and help with cleanup."

A sigh left my mouth as my feet cursed me for all the standing. "Thank God for all these volunteers."

She winked. "Exactly."

The community center was only the *start* of our day. We still had a dinner with her family and dessert with mine. Agreeing to the terms she proposed seemed like a good idea at first. But as we drove across the city to her parents' house, I was starting to think I would have liked to take a nap.

As we neared her house Leah said, "Okay, it's been a while since my parents have met my..." There was a long pause. "Met anyone I was dating."

My grip on the steering wheel tightened and I felt my jaw tensing. "So," I looked to my side, "they'll be drilling me then?" I laughed. "Your brother wasn't the hardest hurdle?"

She cringed. "That'd be my daddy."

"Daddy Moore out here throwing blows?"

She pointed to her house, and I pulled up to the curb. "Brace yourself," she warned before I opened the car door.

Leah unlocked the front door and led us through the house

with a mini tour as we made our way to the kitchen. "And this is where all the action is happening today."

The smells from the kitchen added to the grumbling in my stomach. I thought it was difficult being in the kitchen at the community center most of the day. Serving people and watching them eat was tough. I should have planned a snack at some point.

"Mama," Leah said in a warm tone to the woman standing in front of the stove, "This is Deshaun."

I knew exactly who Leah inherited her looks from. Leah was a stunning resemblance of her mother—same gorgeous smile, big brown eyes, and round face. The only difference between the two was that Mrs. Moore wasn't rocking her hair in long curls. She had a short pixie cut, one that made her grays distinguishable.

"Deshaun." She rubbed her hands across her apron. "Happy for you to join us."

"Thank you for allowing me to stop in." I held my hand out for her to shake, but she opened her arms and embraced me.

She pulled back and patted my shoulder. "We can eat now that we are all here. Grab those dishes," she told Leah. "If you don't mind, Deshaun, grab the others."

I grabbed the dishes and followed Leah into the dining room. When we returned to the kitchen, Leah introduced me to her father.

"Deshaun." He stared at me for a minute. "Nice to meet you."

Unlike her mom, he accepted my outstretched hand. A tight grip around it as he shook. I straightened my back when he finished and looked at him knowingly. I shook hands during many deals, and that extra tight grip said much about the relationship.

We were all seated around the table when her dad showed his cards. After grace and a scoop of potatoes filled my mouth, he said, "I hear you are the one who fired my baby." He had a scorned look on his face.

I swallowed the scoop of potatoes, leaving my mouth uncomfortably dry. I had to sip my water before responding, "Unfortunately, that would be me. It didn't take long before I learned the error in my ways. It's something we are still recovering from at Bryer."

He grumbled. "She's still recovering too." His eyes were on Leah, who was avoiding all eye contact. "Bouncing back from months without a salaried position is a large undertaking."

I cleared my throat, wishing I'd sucked down the glass of water instead of sipping it.

"But she's done it with grace," her mama interjected. "So, tell me, what church do you attend, Deshaun?"

I hoped that either Leah or Liam would contribute to the conversation. I was both hungry and ready to eat, and tense from the questions. The house wasn't hot, but it felt like my shirt was sticking to me. I pulled at it a few times before saying, "I don't have a church." I put a finger between my collar and my neck to stretch out my shirt.

"Seems like an easy solution," her dad offered. "Are you a Christian?"

Liam coughed across the table and Leah gasped.

"Daddy," Leah said with her eyes on him. "Don't do that."

"I can't ask the man dating my daughter if he's a Christian? Seems like important information to me." He frowned as he took a bite of his food.

I also shoved a bite into my mouth, hoping they'd relax on the questions if they saw my mouth full. In all the rooms I'd been inside, none made me as uncomfortable as Leah's dining room.

"I am a Christian," I told him after chewing. "After a recent visit with Leah to her church, I plan to go more often."

"For her or for you?" His questions felt like they were firing at me, and there was nothing I could do to dodge them.

"For me, sir." I felt confident in my response.

Her mom was nodding, and I hoped she understood. She offered, "As long as you know your relationship with God is between you and Him. You shouldn't use it as a token of affection for someone else."

"I agree, Mrs. Moore." I was talking to her but looking at her husband. "The sermon that Sunday was encouraging and uplifted me. It was something I didn't realize I was missing in my life. I appreciate that your daughter was the one to invite me."

Leah stopped cutting into her turkey and placed her knife down.

"I care for your daughter immensely." My eyes connected with Leah's and her lips parted. If we weren't sitting among her family, I would have taken her lips in mine.

"That's good to hear, Deshaun. I'm going to trust the worst thing that will ever come from you is already behind her." Mr. Moore stared at me with his hands propped in front of him.

"Yes sir."

"Alright." Liam clapped his hands. "Now that you've scared the life out of him," we all laughed, "let's enjoy this meal Mama cooked."

I listened to stories of Leah from childhood. They had her

shaking her head and rolling her eyes while the rest of us laughed.

When it was time for us to go to my parents' house, I hoped she'd feel as welcomed as I did. "I like your family," I said, opening her car door.

"Even my dad?" She tilted her head to the side.

I laughed. "Even him. He wants the best for you. I can't be mad about that."

"I guess you're right." Her smile was subtle and hardly noticeable as she sat in the passenger seat.

TWENTY-THREE

Leah

We were on a marathon of a day. And it ended at his parents' house. My hands gripped the passenger seat as he navigated the city between my parents and his.

"I hope you aren't as tense as I was rolling up to your parents' house." There was a smile that accompanied that, otherwise I would have taken it as complete sarcasm.

I didn't tell him I could taste the bile rising through my throat. Or that my heart was beating so hard it felt like it was coming out of my chest. There was even the pounding sound in my ears. "Did you not sit through the agonizing questioning of my dad?" I cringed. "I could hardly sit through it, and he is *my dad.*" I sighed. "I don't know if I can go through anything like that."

"It won't be that bad. I'm sure." His shoulders were back, his head was high. He looked confident, but still I didn't believe his family wouldn't throw a curve ball I wasn't prepared to catch.

"Did they not ask about me coming over?" I wagged my head. "Like what it meant for *us*?" No matter how hard I tried to convince my parents, they insisted that's not what *friends* did for the *holidays*. I had to agree, after we sat down for dinner. Especially after Deshaun's confession that he had intense feelings for me.

My mind was racing a million thoughts a minute. But as we approached a gated entrance, I asked, "Is this their community?" The manicured lawns as he drove a narrow road were beautiful.

He shook his head. "Not exactly." He stared ahead as an illuminated house came into view. "This is their house."

"Where you grew up?" The sheer size of the house was overwhelming. I could only imagine whatever was on the other side of the large oak doors was as lavish.

Deshaun said, "For a large part of my life, yes." He wagged his head. "We moved here when I was about to go to middle school. I've told them they should downsize now that we are all out of the house."

I scoffed. "This is amazing." I shouldn't have expected anything less. Our first date was on a private jet. Before pulling up to the house, I didn't consider his family business was as successful as his.

Staring up at the expansive house was humbling. My parents' house could have fit into one side of theirs.

"Are you okay?" he asked.

I tore my gaze away from the house. "Yes," I told him. "Let's go in."

Loud music and chatter greeted us. Deshaun led us toward

the talking. The chatter as we approached stilled, almost like they were expecting us. We stood at the entrance with all eyes on us.

"Hope you haven't had dessert yet," Deshaun boasted. It was a tone I hadn't heard before. Something lighthearted and carefree.

An older woman who resembled him enough stood from the table. She said, "We've been waiting on you." Her eyes flickered to someone who resembled her more than Deshaun did. "Bianca, come help me." Looking toward Deshaun, she directed, "Go ahead and introduce us so I can steal her away." She looked like she stepped off a photoshoot. Her hair was perfectly curled. Makeup applied with precision. And the dress she wore looked like it'd take at least two of my paychecks to buy. Still, the smile on her face was inviting.

Deshaun looked at me and said, "Mama, everyone, this is Leah. And Leah, this is my family."

I made eye contact with everyone around the table as he introduced them one by one. My eyes faltered on the man seated next to his sister as his name wasn't announced. Deshaun didn't even fake like he knew the man's name.

"This is Carl," his sister said with a smack of her lips.

I assumed, like me, Carl was new to the family gatherings.

"Great," his mama interjected, "Now that's out the way." She walked over and reached for my hand. "Girls, come with me."

Tiana, the woman next to his brother, stood along with us.

Mrs. Green's hand tightened around mine as she led us all toward the kitchen. "I'm excited to have you here with us tonight. Wish you could have arrived earlier. I understand you volunteered and visited with your family first." She dropped my hand to pat my shoulder. "What a long day."

"A long day indeed." I sighed. "But a good one."

The Greens' kitchen was something out of a magazine. A large stovetop, expansive countertops. Even the refrigerator made my mouth gape open. "Beautiful kitchen," I said, turning my head around to see the cabinets that surrounded us.

"Have a seat, honey," his mama said as she went toward an industrial-sized coffee machine. "I'll brew us a pot of coffee."

His sister sat beside me. "I want to know all about you. Don't hold anything back." Her hand cradled her chin as she waited for me to spill my life story.

"Okay, well, I'm in marketing." My hands felt sweaty as I decided on the parts of my life I wanted to share with her, with them. "I graduated from A&T, and my family is from Greensboro. Been here my whole life." I looked beyond Bianca to Tiana, who swiped a cookie from a nearby tray.

"Want one?" she asked as she bit into it.

Bianca's eyes rolled, but she didn't even look over her shoulder. "That's the basics. Tell me how you met Deshaun." Before I could respond, she said, "He's a tough nut to crack. I'm surprised anyone would agree to join him anywhere." She laughed.

"Bianca." His mom's voice was scornful as she put coffee mugs on the counter in front of us. "Your brother is a great guy."

Bianca didn't look convinced. Telling her, "You're his mama." She laughed. "If you didn't believe he was great then he'd really be bad off. But any other person in this world would have a hard time agreeing." She waved her hand in the air.

"But I'll reserve my judgment until I hear how the two of them met."

I cringed, my nose scrunched up and the back of my neck had a layer of sweat on it too. "Well..."

All eyes were on me as I hesitated. Trying to find the best way to tell them he fired me.

I settled on, "It was a rocky meet." I smirked. "Not something we'd share."

"Oh?" His mama looked up. "I thought the two of you met at Bryer."

"You work for him?" Bianca barked, and Tiana looked at me with her eyes wide.

"No. I've never worked for him." I wagged my head. "When he acquired Bryer, he fired me."

There was a collective gasp around the counter, and all eyes went from wide to narrowed. Bianca pointed to Mrs. Green. "See, I told you." She hunched her shoulders. "Deshaun is something else." But then her eyes narrowed as she looked at me. "But you came here anyway? You're dating him?" She rolled her eyes and crossed her arms across her chest.

I laughed. I couldn't even control the laughter coming out of my mouth. It roared so loud it made my stomach ache. "Yeah, I guess I am," I said once the laughter stopped. "He hasn't been as bad since."

Bianca's lips were twisted. "I don't think I'd be able to give Carl the same level of grace." She shook her head. "Nope. If he showed out when we met, I would have left him right where he stood."

Mrs. Green turned with the coffee pot, filling each mug. "See, that's why you need to come with me to church more often. You don't understand the power of forgiveness."

Bianca's eyes widened as she looked toward the ceiling.

"Leah," Mrs. Green handed me a mug of coffee, "I bet you are a regular in somebody's Sunday service, right?" A satisfied smile lifted her lips.

I felt bad that she was using me as a pawn against Bianca. If his mama was anything like mine, I knew it was important to have her kids in church. I responded, "I am." I looked deep into my mug and was ready for the conversation to change.

"See." Mrs. Green handed the other mugs to Bianca and Tiana before pouring others. "Stick around this one. You can already see her sweet ways are rubbing off on Deshaun."

I hadn't considered that. He did serve in the kitchen earlier that day and spoke with members of the community. Then took all the questions from my dad like a champ. I couldn't imagine how he would have responded if his sister was right.

I followed the women from the kitchen to the dining room where each of the guys received a mug of coffee of their own. His mama sat out a tray of cookies and slices of cake.

Deshaun observed the selection in front of him before his eyes landed on mine. His eyebrows bunched before he whispered, "You okay?"

With a hand on his knee, I said, "I am."

Mrs. Green announced, "I love this girl." Her eyes were on me before she looked across the table. "Both of them. They are coming into your lives at a perfect time too." She clapped her hands together and her smile grew even wider. "Your father and I can't wait to spoil some grandbabies."

Deshaun's eyes were as wide as mine felt, and they felt like they stretched to the max. Prepping my parents for Deshaun joining us looked a lot like me telling them we'd been on a few dates, that I liked him. Nothing more, nothing less. *What'd he tell his parents?* I was staring at the side of his face, waiting for him to inform them save the dates had yet to go in the mail. From the way his mama was going on, it was like he'd already proposed and I was weeks away from walking down the aisle.

I let my hand slip from his knee as I picked up a crumb of cake from my plate. If I focused hard enough on the cake, the conversation could wrap up without me giving any input.

Deshaun cleared his throat, and it was like an angel's harp. He said, "Slow down, Mama." He adjusted in his seat. Then placed a napkin across his emptied plate. "We aren't exactly close to *that stage yet.*"

His emphasis made me cringe as I waited for his mama to respond. It wasn't the way I would have phrased it, but at least he said something to stop the tirade his mama was on.

Mr. Green's voice seemed to echo even louder when he spoke. "I wouldn't mind traveling a bit with my wife before we get stuck on grandparent duty."

Laughter filled the room, and from me it was nothing but a nervous reaction. I looked across the table at Tiana to see if she was having a comparable reaction. She was concentrating on the cookie she had in her hand like it was the best thing she ever ate.

"Okay, okay." Mrs. Green wobbled her head. "We'll enjoy a little retirement before we hound you all for babies." Her coffee mug hovered as she asked, "Do you all remember..." That started a long line of stories. Everyone around the table added details.

I stifled a few yawns before I looked at Deshaun. "We should get going before these yawns get disrespectful."

As he stood, Mrs. Green said, "Leah, you can come over whenever you like."

"I'd enjoy that," I replied. Although it was one of the longest days I'd had in a while, I left the Greens' estate feeling like the day was well spent.

I eased into the passenger seat and rested against the headrest. "What a day." My eyes closed as Deshaun pulled away from the house.

"It was everything." I felt his hand on my thigh. "Thanks again for joining me." Once we were on the main road he said, "I've never seen my mother that eager."

I twisted my head so I could watch his silhouette in the dark of the night. "Tell me again the last time you brought a woman home."

His delayed answer made me think about the last guy I brought home to meet my parents. "Never," he said under his breath.

"Never?" I sat up in the seat and my entire body turned toward him. "That's why she's eager. She thinks we are going down the aisle." I watched his face as he looked unbothered by my outburst. "Why me then? We are hardly a couple."

"Would it be bad if we were working toward that?"

I admitted, "I enjoy spending time with you. My initial assessment of you was too harsh."

"Is that right?" He looked at me with a playful grin on his face.

"If nothing else, it's fair if we continue getting to know each other."

"That's fair." His lip curled into his mouth.

He pulled the car into my parents' driveway. "Is it also fair to kiss someone you are getting to know more, because—"

I leaned over the console and pressed my lips against his. His hand curved around my neck and that kiss was more satisfying than all the others. We were in front of my parents' house though, so, I pulled away. "Those kisses are especially of interest to me."

He licked his lips and said, "Me too."

TWENTY-FOUR

Deshaun

Coco was trailing behind me as I walked to my office. But as I got closer to the creative team, their conversation grew louder and louder. I stopped, and Coco bumped into my back. "Coco, back up," I barked as I looked over at the team huddled around one another.

I stood listening as they went back and forth, shouting something about a client.

"It wouldn't surprise me if he didn't have notes on this one too."

I turned to Coco behind me and tilted my head.

"This used to be her client." That part wasn't as loud as the other comments made before I walked up, but it was the one that had me most intrigued.

"What are you discussing?" I eyed each of the team members corralled in the small cubicle space. Margot's eyes grew wide as she watched me. Out of everyone standing there, she had the most to say.

As much as she had to say before, she didn't respond. Not a single word departed her lips. I widened my stance and repeated myself. I addressed her in case there was any confusion who I expected to speak. "Margot, what are you discussing?"

"Mr. Green," her eyes traveled the others around her, "can we speak in your office?"

"Come with me," I said as I stormed toward my office.

"But Mr. Green," Coco shouted behind me, "you have a meeting starting soon."

"It can wait." I stepped a few feet into my office before I told Margot, "You have fifteen minutes." I wrapped my arms across my chest.

"We lost another client." The next words that came from Margot's mouth stalled. Her lips were moving but I couldn't hear anything.

I waved my hand in front of her. "Okay, and what else?" I pointed to my door. "That argument out there felt like there was much more than your team not being able to perform, again." I huffed. The last thing I needed was more bad news.

For two weeks I traveled between my other offices. Each one was performing well. As expected. But because Bryer was doing bad, it was starting to impact the other agencies.

"Brown Brothers won the client." Margot's gaze drifted toward her feet.

"And you don't seem surprised." Brown Brothers' track record was outpacing my expectations. But the news still surprised me. I expected at some point Jacob and his team would lose their momentum.

"I'm not. Not exactly." Her fingers toyed in front of her. "I believe," she looked beside her at Coco, "they have access to notes that we, as an agency, provided about the client. Creative direction."

Coco was tapping on her tablet while Margot spoke. Not once did her head lift though. *Was I the only one shocked by the revelation?*

As Margot continued, none of it was computing. "It'd give them access to details they wouldn't normally have."

I frowned. "That's presumptuous." My eyes narrowed further. "Why is this something you'd even consider?" Margot's delayed response had my blood boiling. "You have something." I held my hands up. "What is it?"

"Someone who was once on our team inquired about it." Margot's shoulders slumped, and she eyed the seats in front of my desk.

But I wasn't worried about her comfort or the stress she appeared to be going through. I needed to know more about what she was saying.

I scoffed. "As in this person knows for a fact that Brown Brothers has these details?" I laughed and shook my head as I pointed to her. "And they told you?"

"She was going to get more details but has since said she can't figure it out. How they'd be able to have access to our notes."

Coco's voice felt like an unwelcomed intruder in the room when she broke the silence. "Your meeting. Five minutes."

My eyes cut toward her, and I said, "It can wait." I looked at Margot. "Thank you for this information. I've got it from here." The door was still open, and I waited for her to leave. "Coco, close the door," I instructed as I turned toward my bookcase. Jacob having our notes would explain a lot. Why would he work against me though? Why wouldn't he be the first to alert me of the breach?

I slammed my fist against the desk. "How would he get access to our notes?"

"I'm looking at the records now." Coco's voice was measured, patient even. She was much calmer than I was in that moment.

I wiped a hand across my face. "Margot has to be mistaken." The beat of my heart was pounding hard against my chest. "It would explain how bad we are doing, but not Jacob." My words trailed before I told her, "Cancel my next meeting. I'm going over there." I crossed my office and was about to walk out the door.

"Wait." Coco's voice was louder. "The only person who used to be here, and is now there is..."

I didn't need Coco to finish her sentence. My hand gripped around the doorknob. I'd spent weeks getting to know Leah. Hours upon hours of conversations with her. Not once did she mention anything about Jacob having the notes.

"Think she's involved?"

With a scowl on my face, I said, "No," and walked out the door.

My hands tightened into a fist as I left the building. The throbbing of my heart was making my head hurt. I climbed into my car and gripped the steering wheel before shouting, "I can't believe this." I pounded my fist into the console.

I needed to be level-headed and calm by the time I reached Jacob. I stared ahead at the road and let the sounds of cars passing focus my attention. Jacob and I had our fair share of fights as kids. Over the ball on the court. Playing video games.

The arguments would always blow out of control before a parent would have to separate us.

I gripped the steering wheel a little harder. There was no way whatever I had to say could blow up like that. By the time I pulled into a parking spot in front of Brown Brothers, I had sore, red palms. Before stepping out of the car, I told myself, "This is a misunderstanding." And because I didn't have all the facts, I convinced myself that's exactly what my friend would say to my face. That there was no way they viewed the notes, even if they did have access to them. That every client they won, they did so honestly.

I walked into the building. Rode the elevator to the tenth floor, and by the time I passed his receptionist that's what I believed.

"Mr. Green," she shouted behind me.

"I need to speak to Jacob." I continued beyond her. "This can't wait." I walked down the long hallway to his office and didn't stop to look for Leah. I needed to see Jacob first.

His office door was open, and he held a phone to his ear. "Deshaun?" He stood from his desk. "What's up?" He scoffed. "I know it's only you. But my receptionist needs to do a better job of letting anybody roll up in here without warning me first."

"Let me call you back," he said into the phone. "How can I help you?" He held his hand out for me, but I didn't shake it.

I pointed to the seat across from him and sat down. "You might want to sit for this." I crossed a leg over my knee. "Jacob, if you were anyone else this conversation wouldn't be this hard."

His voice was shaky as he asked, "What's going on?"

"Do you have access to the Bryer client files?"

His head jerked back, and I noticed a flinch in his eye. It wasn't as bad as it did when we were kids. Not when he was lying to one of our teachers or our parents. But it was noticeable.

"Why would I have access to your client files?"

"From what I understand, your team has access to notes that derived at Bryer."

He sat back in his seat and crossed his arms over his chest. A smug look on his face when he said, "Considering we have a member of your old team." He shifted forward and picked up the phone from his desk. "Let's see what she has to say about this." He watched me before dialing. "Unless you'd prefer for me to not call her in."

"Go right ahead." If it involved her, I wanted to know. I needed to know. I was hoping I'd walk out of that office aware of the mistake, with everything being a huge coincidence.

He hunched a shoulder. He dialed, spoke low into the speaker, then said, "She'll be right in," before hanging up the phone.

With my recent travel schedule, it had been a couple of weeks since I last saw Leah. I was mad about sitting in Jacob's office to discuss the possibility of him stealing from me. But I couldn't be mad about seeing Leah in the middle of the day. There was a light tap at the door before she stepped through. She was wearing a royal blue dress that exemplified her curves. I stared at the heels as she shifted side to side.

"Is everything okay?"

My eyes scanned her body before our eyes met. I wanted to tell her everything was okay, but under the circumstances I kept my mouth shut.

Jacob stood from behind his desk. "It's been brought to my

attention that some of the Bryer client files we've obtained have Bryer notes in them." Jacob looked at me. "You were once a Bryer employee, my only guess is that you have something to do with that."

She didn't speak at first. That didn't stop me from staring at her. Watching her nose as it flared, her eyes as they stared at Jacob like she wanted to cut him in half. If we weren't in that situation, in the middle of that conversation, I would have asked her what that was all about. Instead, I watched, waited for her to respond to him.

"Ms. Moore, do you have an answer?"

I cleared my throat and told Jacob, "Be easy."

The first word out of Leah's mouth brought my attention back to her.

"That's correct. Some of the files I have seen do have notes from Bryer."

It was like she was delivering a weather report or consulting him on an email. Not like she was admitting that she knew his company had notes from Bryer.

I looked between the two of them with my eyebrows stitched together. "What?"

Jacob's hands went into the air. "Let me tell you this, if I find out you have used those notes to garner favor with old clients, you are out of here." His face didn't wrinkle, didn't show a sign of distress. "I will work with our team to figure out how we are even able to access the notes." He waved his hand toward the door. "Leah, get back to work."

Before walking out, I watched her bite the side of her lip.

Jacob had a sly smile on his face when he announced, "There you have it. That should settle it."

I widened my stance to issue a warning. "Jacob, as a business associate, I trust your intentions are to operate above board, and fairly. That your business ethics are beyond reproach." I tightened my jaw. "As a longtime friend, I expect you'd at least respect me. Enough not to use something that would put you at an unfair advantage against *me.*"

He sucked his teeth and held his hands in front of him. "Deshaun." His head tilted to the side. "Of course not, man." He wagged his head. "But if I do find out Leah is on some revenge kick, I'll handle that accordingly. Can't have folks out here going rogue. Right?"

"Right," I repeated before retreating from his office. I needed to leave before I said something that would issue the final dagger to our friendship. Or whatever remained of it.

As my steps neared Leah's desk, I slowed. The sting I felt addressing her was worse than it felt with Jacob. "Leah. You knew all along?"

"It's not what you think." She shook her head. She looked from me to her laptop. "But I shouldn't say anything else in here."

"If you know something," I felt my voice waver, "tell me."

She closed her eyes and when she re-opened them she said, "Ask your team. They might have more details."

I wanted to ask her to follow me out. But we were in an awkward situation. "Okay," I told her before leaving the office. I left feeling more conflicted about the situation than when I entered.

TWENTY-FIVE

Leah

In a few short minutes, everything I gained was in danger. I couldn't even look at Deshaun. Not when he was looking at me like I slighted him in the worst way possible. In a way, I did. I should have told him everything I knew when I found out.

I trusted Jacob when he said he had no idea what was going on. But he threw me under the bus like I was the one in the wrong. That wasn't expected, at all.

Reciting, "God give me strength," was the only thing that kept me from losing my job that day. I was close to giving Deshaun the play-by-play of the conversation I had with Jacob. To watch Jacob recover from that revelation. But I didn't. I trusted that God would come through again.

It didn't stop me from whispering silent prayers all the way to the conference room for my meeting though. Everyone on my team was still in the colleague category. None of them were anyone I was comfortable with complaining to. I took a long deep breath and stepped into the conference room.

I was calm sitting at the table until I heard, "Okay team," and watched Jacob step to the front of the room.

The eyes around the table glanced around the room. Jacob's attendance wasn't normal. He never sat in on our meetings. It didn't help that he was at the front of the room, making an announcement.

The last time I was in the conference room feeling that uneasy, it ended terribly bad. *God, please don't let this end up like that.*

"I want to remind each of you what we do inside this building is confidential." Jacob was leaning on the conference room table watching us. "Don't share it under any circumstances." His eyes landed on me. "Especially with anyone at another agency. If there is any doubt about what will happen, review your employment contract."

We were on the receiving end of confidential information. So, I didn't think the announcement was relevant.

My boss, Denise, asked, "Mr. Brown, is there something we should be aware of?"

Jacob sighed a long-exaggerated breath. "We are being accused of stealing ideas from another agency here in the city." There wasn't much of a shocked response around the table. "I want to prevent unwarranted rumors." After Jacob left the room, everyone started chatting.

Denise didn't interrupt and started whispering herself. After a little back and forth, she stood in front of the room. "Let's proceed with the agenda."

"Yes, please," I said a little louder than anticipated.

The topic of stealing wasn't discussed further, but it was far from gone in my mind. I left work that day even more determined to figure out who was responsible.

Hectic days reminded me I didn't have privacy at home. If I did have my own place, I would have gone straight to the bathroom and run a hot bubble bath. But because I didn't, I walked into the kitchen and turned on the tea kettle. A hot cup of tea would have to suffice.

Before I could sit down with my mug, my mama entered the kitchen. One look at me and she asked, "Leah, what's wrong?"

I blew the steam from my mug and said, "I messed up," and my shoulders slumped.

Her face twisted up. "What do you mean?"

I started to explain the situation with Deshaun. About the notes I found months prior. The conversation with Jacob and Margot. How I didn't tell Deshaun I knew about the notes, then finally, "Today Deshaun came into Brown Brothers."

"Do I need a cup of tea?" she asked, eyeing mine.

I smirked. "Maybe."

She walked to the kettle and filled it with water. "Leah, sounds like a mess. What are you going to do?"

All the issues, all the things that needed fixing came flooding my mind. "There's so much," I told her. "How do I even start?"

"The files. Prove you didn't steal the notes." Then her lip worried between her teeth. "But, if they are your notes anyway, would it matter? You had the ideas in the first place, right?"

I wagged my head. "I mean, yes. But no. It would matter. But I mean in this case, it's not me who even used the notes. The way it looks to me is that someone is using the notes to gain the client. I'm not even contributing to the conversation."

She pulled her mug to her face. "Okay. How do you prove that?"

"I don't know, but I feel obligated to do so."

Her slender finger rose in the air. As it shook, she said, "No." She huffed. "We think control is a worthy trait, but it's more admirable to seek help when things are beyond your control." She lowered her finger and tapped the counter. "We like to be independent to a fault. We want everything to go our way and expect everything and everyone else will bend in our favor, that's not reality." She smiled. "It's also a good reminder that we need to illicit God more in our daily walk. So much is out of our control, and often we are looking in the wrong place for help."

I assured her, "I prayed for His help."

"And do you trust He will give it to you?"

"Well," I started, "Of course. Otherwise, I wouldn't have prayed."

She shook her head. "Faith is a belief system. Trust is an action."

I refuted, "It seems like the one lesson I learned over this year." I sighed. "Wish I wasn't back learning another one this soon," I told her, "Mama, Deshaun looked like he lost all trust in me."

Mama's encouraging words took a while to frame. "When

Deshaun first approached you, you had your reservations, right?"

There were a few hurdles I had to overcome when we first met. One being that he fired me. Another being that he was wealthy. The most important was he didn't seem like the nicest guy to be around.

"And over time your thoughts changed, right?"

It took some time but when he broke through my wall, it came crashing down.

"It may not be overnight, but if you've done nothing else to put your trust into question, he'll come around."

"Until then?" I cocked my head toward her as her hand stroked mine.

"You put your trust in God. That He will straighten your path. Give you a way forward."

My shoulders eased down from my ears. "Thanks, Mama."

"Anytime, baby." She wrapped an arm around my shoulder and tucked me into her side. "Leah, I pray everything works out the way you want, but most of all, the way God intends it to."

TWENTY-SIX

Deshaun

I stared out the window of my office, in the middle of the day, in the middle of the week. It wasn't like me to feel deflated. But I was rolling around on four flats.

As a cloud parted in the sky, I closed my eyes and said, "God." I leaned forward and dropped my head. It'd been so long since I'd open that line of communication with Him I didn't know what to say. I needed a divine power to step in and work a miracle. At least that's what I was feeling as I sat there in my office.

A notification alerted me to an upcoming meeting. I turned my seat around and stared at my laptop. I wasn't prepared. I should have spent the morning going over the client notes and reviewing the creative team's pitch. Instead, my head was in the clouds.

A light knock at the door preceded Coco peeking her head through the crack. "Mr. Green?"

I waved my hand. "Come in."

She pulled her tablet in front of her. Without hesitation, she started reading the bullets for the meeting. Her eyes rose from the list. "What happened?" She looked over my shoulder then back to me. "You haven't stopped me once. You've never not stopped me."

My shoulders hunched. "I'm at odds with my best friend. And the woman I was falling for could be to blame," I huffed. "Seems more than enough to have me feeling stuck."

With a blank stare on her face, she said, "I get it. But you didn't return to Greensboro for none of that, right?"

I raised my hand in front of me but couldn't deny what she was saying.

"The way I see it, the show must go on." She snapped her fingers. "If you can pull this client, you won't have to worry about either of them." Her tablet lifted in front of her again.

What did it matter what Coco thought? I'd never heard of her speaking of a friend. Let alone anyone she was close with outside of work. And a partner? Would she even know the weight of having someone close betray her?

I wanted Bryer to be successful, but at what cost? At one point, there wasn't anything I wouldn't do to be successful, but that didn't seem to matter much anymore. Finding that balance between a business life and personal one felt significant. It wasn't something I was ready to surrender.

But as Coco stood in front of me waiting, I knew she was the last person I could get to understand. "Alright, proceed," I told her.

She did so with enthusiasm. "Your creative team is ready

to discuss the prospective client." Then she ended it with, "I'll meet you in the conference room. Need anything?" Her back was toward me as she asked.

"I could use a cup of coffee."

She offered to run and grab it, and I remembered the little coffee shop next door. How running into Leah that day was the catalyst to everything that was now happening. That sweet, caring, giving person couldn't be the person that would deceive me, lie to me, steal from me. There was no way she had anything to do with the notes.

She told me to ask my team, but I didn't think I could trust any of them. I couldn't imagine anyone had anything to gain by helping our competitors. Not when their performance would take a hit at Bryer.

I rubbed my hand across the stubble on my face and tried once more to pull on God for help. "God," my head bowed and eyes closed, "I need your help. I'm sure there is a lot I haven't done to please you over the years. And I pray you'll forgive me. But please help me." I sniffed and raised my head before remembering, "Amen."

I stood from my desk and felt no more equipped than I did before I prayed. But my shoulders straightened and head lifted. Regardless, if God was going to help me or not, I had to push forward.

The conference room was full of the creative team ready to hear about our prospective client. Eyes were wide and watching, but before I gave them details about the client, I said, "I need you to do one thing." My eyes scanned the table. Margot focused on me most, and I questioned whether she could be the cause of the leak.

"Scrub all the notes from this client. Don't use any of it for the pitch. I want you to start fresh, from scratch."

Margot sat up in her seat and said, "That'll take more time than we have. When we have a new client, we use the notes from sales to form the creative. Without it, we'll have to gather details ourselves before we can even start."

"Pull whatever resources you need." I leaned on the table and eyed her. "You are the creative team. If you can't find a creative solution to this challenge, I question whether you're doing your job anyway."

Margot's head jilted back, and she scoffed. "Of course, we can find a creative solution." She looked around the table. "But the question isn't what we can create. It's if we will have time to do so."

"Unfortunately, we don't have that luxury." I wagged my head. "The alternative is handing this client over to a competitor. And that's something that we can't afford anymore."

The new notes could still get compromised though, and that was more of a problem than them using old notes. "I'll work to ensure the files have limited access."

Coco walked in with a cup of coffee outstretched to me. "Did I miss anything?" She took a seat and opened her tablet.

"I'm explaining a plan to ensure our files are not compromised. Take the rest of the day to brainstorm ideas." I believed the team could win the client. With a fair opportunity they could succeed. After all the losses we took, we needed it.

As I left the conference room, Coco trailed me. "I didn't realize you were thinking of a plan to protect the files."

I looked over my shoulder. "Why wouldn't I?" I straightened my back. "Coco." I narrowed my eyes at her. "I'm not in this business to lose."

She blurted, "Of course not." She stopped at her desk. "If there is any way I can help, let me know." Her smile tightened.

"I'll let you know." I stepped toward my office. "I'm headed out for the day."

"Already?"

"I have some other business to tend to." I walked into my office to gather my laptop. Afterward, I said, "Have a good evening."

Christmas was around the corner. My mom called that morning letting me know that she was baking cookies for the neighbors. She asked if I would join her. At first, it was an immediate no. But as the day wore on, the thought of cookies was brightening my day.

On the drive from the office to their house, I made a mental list of all the possible people who could be behind the leak. *Jacob, Margot, someone in IT*. I cringed as I added one more person, *Leah*. It'd been a couple of days since our encounter at Brown Brothers. Each time I picked up the phone to call her something urged me to put it back down. At the same time, my phone wasn't ringing with her on the other end either.

I pulled into my parents' driveway and shook off the day. Shook off everything about the leak. Everything about Leah. I needed a break from the challenges.

When I walked inside the house, the smell of cookies brought a smile to my face. Had my stomach doing flips. "Ehm, I hope you baked a pan for me," I announced as I walked into the kitchen.

"Deshaun?" Mama turned from the sink. "What are you doing here?"

Laughing, I said, "You invited me." I looked at the stacks of cookies already on the counter. "And after some thought, I decided I could volunteer my services." I tapped my stomach. "Taste tester extraordinaire."

She smirked. "You've been volunteering down at the community center. Now that helping spirit has taken root in your soul." She eyed me. "Told your sister Leah was rubbing off on you. When you said 'no' earlier, I knew you wouldn't leave me hanging." She waved her hand. "And look at God." Her arms stretched out wide and we embraced.

Through the hug, and the smell of buttery goodness on her skin, I couldn't ignore the reminder she gave me. "Not sure Leah is the one that spreads goodness." I looked down at Mama's head.

"What happened?" Her lips curved to the side as she pulled away. The look she gave me was total disbelief. Like Leah could do no wrong.

"I think," I started and tried to find the words, "she's been helping Brown Brothers steal clients from us."

She gasped, and her response was exactly how I felt thinking about the situation. But then she shook her head. "No." She shook her head again. "Not Leah. She doesn't have a bad bone in her body."

"That we've seen." As much as I wanted to believe what Mama said, I knew there were people in the world who could deceive. "She has every reason to want revenge."

"She has a good heart, a good spirit. She's a decent person, Deshaun." She had more confidence in Leah than me in that moment.

"And how do you know that. For sure?" I asked her.

"People may be able to act a certain way, but deep down

that doesn't connect. Over time the heart reveals the soul of a person. Their intentions."

"But." Leah in her cubicle looked conflicted. What if that was her heart revealing her true self. "She had the opportunity to explain the situation, she didn't give me much to believe it wasn't her. She told me to ask the people on my team."

"And did you?" Mama's hand was on her hip.

"I don't know if I can trust them."

She smacked her lips and swatted a towel in my direction. "Deshaun, honey, you can't walk around here not trusting anybody."

The added stress wouldn't be good for Mama's heart though, so I told her. "Let's focus on these million cookies you need to bake." Ingredients were all over the kitchen. Cookie tins in every corner of the space.

She grabbed a bowl of mix and said, "Here, start dropping these on that pan." She pointed to a pan tucked away on the counter.

I looked from the pan to her and said, "I planned to eat the cookies. Not exactly help bake them."

"Uh huh." She laughed. "See how the heart works. You revealed you had no intentions of helping me." She winked. "Leah may be loyal to a fault. She could have told you it wasn't her. But it may have revealed something you aren't prepared to hear about your best friend."

"My best friend?" I grabbed the mix from her and dropped a lob of dough on the pan.

Mama started on another batch of mix. She stirred and focused on adding ingredients to the bowl. She glanced at me and said, "Deshaun, I've always been suspicious of Jacob."

Jacob spent countless hours in our house when I was

growing up. I would have never been able to tell that Mama had any issues with him. Not until she reminded me, "Remember when you were a kid, and the two of you would get into trouble? I warned you to be cautious of the company you kept?"

"Yeah. I thought you meant that as a general observation." There were other guys I hung around back then. Not any of them I kept in contact with like Jacob though. And if I had to say whether they were a good influence, or not, I'd err on the side of not.

She chuckled. "I could have been more obvious. I guess." Then she said, "But when it comes to parenting, I couldn't always go for the most direct path." She frowned as her hand continued mixing. "Especially not with you."

There was a lot to unpack there. More than I could conceive in one conversation. "I wish you could have been more direct." Under my breath I said, "It would have been nice to know." I couldn't think of a single time that I suspected Jacob was not trustworthy. Not the times when we were playing sports and on each other's team. Even when we were on opposing teams, still we cheered each other on. If there was a girl I liked, he'd back away when I started getting serious. We helped each other on school projects. And when I started the agency, he was the first person giving me advice on what to do, and not to do.

"If I missed that with Jacob, couldn't I be missing something with Leah too?" I dropped the last of the dough onto the pan and carried it to the oven.

Her tone was strong when she said, "Deshaun, my intuition is telling me you are not. In fact, if there's anyone you can trust in this situation, it's her."

My shoulders slacked as I admitted, "I haven't called her in a few days."

She sighed. "Get those cookies in the oven. It's going to be a long night."

I did as she said, placing the cookies in the oven. Taking the pan that was inside out and resting it on the stove. "Can I try one?" My hand was reaching for a cookie with chocolate oozing from the side.

Mama shook her head and said, "First tell me why you haven't called her."

"I don't know what to say. Not until I know who is responsible, I don't want to act like everything is okay."

She placed a large bowl in front of me, then eyed an empty pan. "Deshaun, you can't stay stuck. You must push forward." The words from earlier in the day stood out like she had highlighted them mid-air. "How will you move forward?"

"For the files I have a plan." My smile dropped. "For Leah, not so much."

"Put in the effort. Figure it out. And whatever you do, don't take too long. She doesn't deserve to be put on the backburner."

"You're right." I looked over at the pan of cookies on the stove and asked again, "How about a cookie now?"

Mama laughed and handed me a warm cookie.

TWENTY-SEVEN

Leah

If I went the rest of my life without another scandal I'd consider myself blessed. I sat in my car outside of the community center with a stack of printed papers. I had to wait until most of the office was clear to sneak them out. Waiting was worth it if I could prove to Deshaun that I wasn't involved in the situation.

Flipping through the files, everything was starting to become a blur. I was standing at the edge of the forest, and I couldn't identify a single tree. *Or however that saying went.*

I rubbed my hand across my eyes and sighed. Something had to give, and soon. There were only a couple of weeks until Christmas. The closer it came the more I prayed I could spend it with Deshaun. But I was starting to lose hope. *Is it God's will?* I looked up at the roof of my car and uttered, "God, I know you can work this out." I stuffed the stack of papers under my seat and stepped out of the car.

Because of the long hours at work, it'd been a while since the last time I stepped inside of the community center. That was another thing that was weighing heavy on me. And since I was counting my offenses, my parents needed help with their bills. Nothing seemed to be going right, when weeks earlier, everything seemed perfect.

That entire year had been a rollercoaster, and I was praying I was at the end of the ride. But as I walked into the community center, a heavy weight greeted me. It reminded me, no matter what, my life was still pretty good.

I met the other volunteers in the kitchen to help carry dishes to the dining room. "Leah," I heard from behind me. The sound of Ms. Carol's voice was a balm to my soul. "How are you, honey?" She walked over to me, examining me from head to toe. "It's been a little while. Everything okay?"

"I've been working late. Super busy at work." My lips lifted into a half-smile. "I was coming tonight to help with the Christmas decorations though." Every year the community center went all out for the members. By all out, I meant they'd decorate with what they had. Some homemade decorations, others donated. We did the most we could with them though.

Ms. Carol stretched her arms out and wrapped me in a hug. "I'm glad you found a way in tonight. Don't let those people stress you out, honey. You know rest is important too."

Oh, how I understood that. "Yes, ma'am."

Before I walked away from Ms. Carol, she blurted, "Should've brought that young man to help." Her eyes were sparkling as she said it too.

I laughed. "Deshaun?"

Her smile was as wide as the sea. "Yes, him."

"Didn't get a chance to invite him." I thought about how he helped for Thanksgiving. How I would have loved to see him hang an ornament or a string of lights.

Ms. Carol sounded as disappointed when she said, "Oh, okay. Well get on to it so you aren't here all night." She patted my arm and left the kitchen.

I walked down the long, dark hallway toward Liam's office. His door was open, but still I knocked before entering. "Liam."

He looked up from his desk. "Leah." His face formed into something I'd never seen before. Something like pure delight. "You won't believe what the director told me."

Considering how the year had been going. The peak of the ride I was on. I cringed waiting for him to deliver bad news. "What?" I didn't have the energy to guess and didn't want to elongate the suspense.

"The center received the largest donation check. Ever." His mouth formed the next words with care. "Like ever."

I clapped. "That's great." I could think of a few ways they could spend the check. "Now you can start knocking out some of the dire needs of this place." Then I narrowed my eyes and asked, "Who was the gift from?" The Christmas season was notorious for gifting. It was when the center received most of their monetary donations each year.

Liam stood from his seat and said, "The person chose to be anonymous."

That sounded appropriate considering a large donation. They wouldn't want everyone knowing how much money they were throwing around.

"I know who it is though." Liam was staring at me as I waited. "Deshaun."

Air caught in my throat, and I coughed. Patting my chest as I shook my head. "Who?"

"Deshaun. Your guy."

I repeated, "Deshaun? My guy?" after the coughing subsided. "Why do you think that?"

He scratched his head. "There was a note." He looked up like it appeared in the space above his head. "It said, 'on behalf of the kindest woman I know, Leah Moore.'" Then he laughed. "Unless you are out here befriending more than one millionaire, then I'd say—"

"But I'm kind to everyone I meet." I could have also explained the situation me and Deshaun were in. The one where my kindness was put to the test. Where he could be thinking I was kind but a liar. But there was an even simpler explanation. "Deshaun isn't the type that would make a donation."

"Even the Tin Woodman found a heart, right?"

I laughed. "What?" Shaking my head, I added, "And we aren't exactly on speaking terms right now."

"If he messed up," Liam offered, "this could be his way of making up for all that."

"Or, it's an end of the year write-off." I laughed. "Not like I'd know anything about having a large sum of money I needed to get rid of." I could think of all the ways I could use extra money.

Liam didn't seem fazed. "Whatever it is, I'm grateful." He went on to tell me how they planned to make use of the donation. "Expand the housing program. Increase meals we serve each night. Outreach to more people who need help. This is going to have a far reach."

"You're right. It's great." No matter how they received the

donation, the result was beneficial. "We should start deco-
rating before it gets too late. Early start for me in the morning."
I tilted my wrist. It was already past eight o'clock.

"Sure." He pointed to a corner of his office. "Those boxes
should have everything we need." I pulled one out and hoisted
it in my arms. "Keep being kind, Leah, the reach is further
than you realize."

I was the one who would give encouraging words, usually.
But in that moment I felt discouraged. My teeth were grinding
before I told Liam, "Except, it misses me. In the situation I'm
in with work, I could be the one who ends up getting burned."

Liam shifted a box to one arm and put his other around my
shoulder. "As long as you're doing what's right, in the end,
God is always on your side." He emphasized, "Anything that
doesn't work out for you wasn't meant for you to begin with."

I laughed. "You swear you are the older one, huh?" But his
wise words were helpful. "I appreciate your optimism."

The dining room was clear of all the members and volunteers. I took to one corner of the room and started assembling
the small tree. Once it was standing, I started hanging ornaments and stringing lights. With each branch I plucked and
fluffed, I thought over the year. How each situation unfolded.
From thinking I'd get promoted, instead fired. Showing up
daily to *Cup of Sunshine,* to working at Brown Brothers. The
scandal. Then, being apprehensive about getting to know
Deshaun, to falling for him.

And now I was somewhere lost amid it all.

I grabbed an angel ornament from the box. I hung it on a
branch, making it visible to everyone who would walk by the
tree. As it dangled in front of me I said, "God, if Deshaun and I
should be together, don't let anything or anyone stand in the

way." I touched the branches around the angel then whispered, "Amen."

Stepping back from the tree, I admired each of the ornaments. The string of lights, and the decorations Liam placed on the tables around the room. "It's beautiful," I whispered. Christmas spirit was ushered in. Although I wouldn't be spending it the way I hoped, I was thankful for all I still had. Good health, a loving family, and a job to pay my bills. I couldn't worry about what would happen in the future. I had to continue trusting no matter what, God would have me.

Liam stood beside me, an arm draped over my shoulder. "As always, Leah, thanks for your help. And, if it was Deshaun or not, I hope whoever made the donation has an amazing Christmas."

My chest heaved before I whispered, "Me too, Liam."

TWENTY-EIGHT

Deshaun

I wanted to spend Christmas with Leah. I wished Jacob could have been at my parents' annual holiday party as always. Not having either put me in a bah humbug spirit. I was ready to sprint into the New Year when it came. I didn't want to waste any time getting back to business. Especially if that meant a new client.

So, when it was time for us to announce the client we had won, I ensured we celebrated big. There were bottles of champagne in the conference room. And we even invited the client in to celebrate with us.

Seeing Coco looking all doom and gloom despite everyone's excitement was surprising. But I shook it off and stood in front of the conference room to congratulate the team.

"Today we celebrate a new partnership." I held up a glass of champagne as I looked around the room. Wide smiles and bright eyes looked back at me. "I'm excited about the opportunity to bring our creativity to your products. What the creative team has dreamed up is nothing short of amazing."

A slow clap started at the back of the room until everyone was clapping along. "Enjoy this celebration, but on Monday, we get to work." I moved around the room until I met Roger, the client's CEO, standing on the other side. "So, tell me, Roger, what was our tipping point?" It was a question our sales team would have asked as a follow-up, but I couldn't wait for those results. I wanted to know now.

After all, Roger's company brought us the largest project in the history of Bryer. Other subsidiaries could follow, and I wanted to ensure we maintained our momentum.

He looked around the room. "If this is appropriate," his eyes narrowed as he lowered his voice, "Brown Brothers didn't know our brand. They didn't know our products well. And the creative showed that." He lifted his glass to his lips, and after a sip he said, "The other agencies didn't come close to you two."

My chest rose as I listened. It was what I always knew about my agency as a whole and was waiting for Bryer to catch up. I was proud they did. Even if it was a struggle to get them there.

Roger smirked. "It's a shame though. They have a super star on their team. She tried hard to present us options that could have worked. But their CEO didn't seem to respect her perspective."

The grip around my glass tightened until the glass shook, dripping champagne on my hand. "Very unfortunate."

He lifted his hand toward my shoulder, and as he tapped it he said, "Your team cares. Top to bottom. And at the end of the day, I want to do business with people who care." He finished his glass of champagne then said, "I should get going. We have some things to get prepared before the kick-off. No time like the present to make sure the team knows the way forward."

"Absolutely." I reached my hand out to him. "My team will be ready as soon as you are."

After Roger and his team exited the conference room, I announced, "Team, again, great work." I left the room, and the celebration.

Brian, from IT, came rushing toward me. "Mr. Green," he said. His face flushed and it looked like the short hallway served as his track. "I need to speak to you." His voice stuttered through heavy breaths.

"Sure." I looked over my shoulder. Brian was responsible for ensuring we locked the files. I had to trust he had no reason to sabotage the company, and that in the least he would help me find who was. "Is everything okay?" After winning the client I assumed we'd see no issues with the files. I assumed whatever Brown Brothers was up to was over.

The look on Brian's face made my heart drop into my stomach. "No." He shook his head as paranoia settled onto his face.

My hand slickened with sweat and my forehead crinkled. "What is it?" I wanted to scream, but I maintained a level voice.

"Can you come with me?" he asked but had turned toward his corner of the floor before I could even respond.

I had to power walk to keep up with his stride. He held his door open for me as I stepped into the darkened room. The door closed behind me, and for a moment I feared what could happen on the other side. It felt like I was entering into a matrix. Computer monitors and machines crowding the small space. The only light coming from the illuminated screens.

"Mr. Green," he said as he took his seat behind his computer. "People we granted access viewed the files." He tapped a few strokes on his keyboard. "Then, I saw this." He pointed to the screen. A string of words highlighted.

I looked from the words to him and waited for him to tell me what the words meant.

"Sent outside of the firewall."

With my hand in the air, I said, "Brian." I stared at the words on the screen again. I needed to catch up to what he was explaining. "What does all this mean?"

He tapped the keyboard more. The screen changed as he did. "It means the file went to someone outside of Bryer."

"Do you know who sent it? And to where?" I felt my veins pulsing and the room grew warmer. I could have stretched out and touched either of the walls, and that was too close. I fanned my face and plucked my collar.

"At first, no." He shook his head. "But then I started to dig, checked IP addresses. The devices accessing them. Verified who is assigned to them."

He was entering into the zone where I no longer followed. I didn't interrupt him though. I hoped the end of his rant would lead me to the answer I'd been searching weeks to find.

"I went a step further and cross-referenced the file with previous files. The leak is all pointing to the same person. Sent to the same network out of Bryer."

Margot, Jacob, Leah... Brown Brothers. I held my fist to my mouth as I anticipated his next words.

"It went to Brown Brothers Agency."

"Right, I expected that."

Brian looked at me with narrowed eyes. "Okay." He explained how he confirmed that detail with a few phone calls. "And Coco sent it."

My head jarred back. "As in my assistant, Coco?" Coco had access to all my files, at all my companies. Never once in the many years she worked with me did I have an issue with her. I was shaking my head as he raised his laptop to my eye level. Another string of words on the screen.

"Right here." He pointed. "This is the data that tells us it is her." Then Brian proved he was more than thorough. "We can check her tablet too." He continued, "The tablet she is always carrying around. It'll confirm. Then if we check her emails, we can see the files leaving our network."

I ran my thumb against my chin. "Are you certain?"

"Yes."

Could the situation get any worse? My assistant and my best friend plotting against me? "Let's verify," I told Brian as I reached for the door. There wasn't anything that Coco would gain by sharing files with Jacob. "Let's go to my office, and I'll call her in."

He followed close behind me as I stalked out of his office on a path to mine. I lifted my phone to my ear and called Coco. "Meet me in my office."

Her voice was shaky when she asked, "Is everything okay?"

"It will be." I was certain of that. One way or another, I'd understand why she'd betray me the way she did. I trusted her with all my business dealings. There had to be a reasonable answer despite the feeling deep in my gut that there wasn't one.

Brian and I entered my office, and I asked him to take a

seat. Coco walked in a few minutes later and looked from me to Brian. As her eyes flickered down to her tablet, I knew the pieces of the puzzle were coming together for her. Her eyes widened at first, then she wiped the emotion from her face. She straightened her back and stared straight at me. Over the years she must have watched me. I took a similar posture when entering negotiations, business deals. *Never show your hand.*

I cleared my throat before I said, "Coco, Brian has discovered how the files leaked. And who has leaked them. Is there a need for us to check your tablet to verify?"

She looked down at the tablet in her hand. She raised it to her chest and said, "No." She looked at Brian then back to me and asked, "Can we speak privately?"

I had the answer I needed. It was Coco. But now I wanted to know the why. "Brian, could you give us a minute?" I watched him stand from his seat and walk toward the door.

"I'll be on standby if you need me." Brian closed the door behind him.

I held my head up toward the ceiling. "Coco," I said, letting my gaze fall to her, "Not a single reason comes to mind about why you'd help Jacob. Why you'd betray me. Why you'd hurt this business. We've worked together for years. Why now?"

Defeat etched over her face as her shoulders slumped. "There shouldn't be one." She admitted, "I got caught up in Jacob's promises."

I crossed my arms over my chest and listened.

"Since the first time you introduced us, he's been in my ear about what the two of us could have. What we could build *together*. Then when we moved here to Greensboro, he became even more persistent." She sighed. "He needed my help to grow his portfolio. Then he'd have leverage to acquire more agencies like you've been doing."

I fell into my seat and held my head between my hands. "Not only was he stealing from me, but he used you to do it. Then he allowed me to think it could be Leah. You..." I looked at her and pointed my hand toward her. "You allowed me to think that was the case."

She snickered. "I believed he had a plan. That I needed to stick to whatever the fall out was so this would all work out." She stepped closer to my desk. "Deshaun, I'm sorry. I know what I've done is beyond repair." She placed her tablet on the edge of my desk. "I can grab my stuff and leave."

I scoffed. Standing, I said, "You're right, this is beyond repair." I took a deep breath and tried to calm my noisy breathing. "Coco, I'm sure there are legal ramifications associated with this."

That initial look of panic I saw when she walked into the room and saw Brian was back. She shook her head. "Deshaun, please."

I raised my hand. "Cooperate with Brian. Assure me there is nothing else at risk for Bryer or my other agencies, and I'll consider bypassing that option. I don't want this to hit the news any more than you do."

"Whatever you need." Her face was back to the stoic look. Of all the years working with me, I wished there was something better she learned from me.

I raced across the city to get to Brown Brothers. I needed to talk to Jacob in person. Before Coco had a chance to give him the details. As angry as I was with Coco, and Jacob, my heart grew softer thinking about Leah.

I owed her an apology. For being in Jacob's web of deceit, and for me not trusting her more. For allowing the situation to grow a wedge between us.

The elevator to the tenth floor wasn't long enough. Not long enough for me to craft the words I wanted to say to Jacob. The elevator doors opened, and I ignored the receptionist as she greeted me.

"Mr. Green," she shouted behind me, "he's in with someone."

Over my shoulder I told her, "Better let him know I'm on my way."

Jacob had no respect for my business, or the people around me. Any ounce of respect I had for his business went out the window after speaking with Coco.

A few feet down the hall, I met a familiar face. "Mr. Green," he said, "good to see you."

He looked over my shoulder as I recognized who he was. A man from a previous pitch.

"Unexpectedly, here." He tilted his head to the side.

"Good to see you." It didn't show in my face and wasn't heard in my tone. I focused on getting to Jacob's office.

I barged through the door and looked at the man seated across from him. "Jacob, we need to speak."

With a smirk on his face, he asked the man to give him a minute. When it was the two of us across from each other, he said, "I'm conducting business. I don't need you barging in on me." He flailed his arm in the air. "What is this about, Deshaun? You won the client, so what are you over here for this time?" He sneered. "You do realize my phone works the same as it has over the years."

I barked, "If only this was something I could discuss over the phone. Believe me, the last place I want to be is here. I have a business of my own to tend to."

"Sounds like it's pointless to you too then."

I wanted to knock the smug look off his face. But in all my years of business, I remained calm. We weren't on the sidelines of the basketball court where he fouled me. We weren't kids running around the house and he blamed me for breaking a vase. We were two adult men, with too much to lose for me to do what I wanted to him.

"Except..." I pointed toward him. "I learned today how you were able to gain confidential information from Bryer." I shook my head. "I'm surprised to hear it, honestly. Moreso, surprised that you went after someone that close to me to get it."

He laughed. "You finally realized Leah was the problem." He reached for his desk phone. "I'll tell her to pack up her stuff."

I walked closer to his desk and placed a hand over the handset. "No." I looked him in the face and said, "Coco." I smirked and watched as his face soured. "Guess you didn't suspect I'd find out," I huffed. "Or that she wouldn't have called to warn you first." I stood with a hand on his desk. "Here's what is going to happen. She's fired. And if I ever have any other issues with you, I'll be sure everyone in this city knows what type of businessman they are dealing with."

I backed away from his desk. "Tell me, Jacob, of all the people in the world you could have taken from, why me?"

He rolled his seat back and steepled his hands on his lap. "You had New York. You could have expanded into any other city." He sucked his teeth. "But you came here. Into my territory." The anger in his eyes matched mine.

When I considered acquiring Bryer, it was to be closer to family. I never imagined he'd consider me inheriting his competition as a threat. The way I saw it, there was enough food for both of us to eat. If we remained the number one and two spot, all else was irrelevant no matter who held first place.

The scowl on his face was deepening.

"Then, instead of rooting for me to win, beside you, you had to knock me down?" I looked over his shoulder to the cityscape outside.

He stood from his seat. "It's all business. *Nothing personal.*"

"For you, maybe," I told him, "I have one other condition. Release Leah from her employee contract. Release her from any non-competes. I want her back at Bryer." I didn't want her to be at risk working for Jacob. I also didn't want him having constant access to her. If he was savage enough to go after Coco, I didn't doubt he wouldn't be trying to claw his way into Leah too.

"That's a no go." His smile was sinister. "She's an asset to my company."

I warned, "There won't be a company once everyone finds out what you've done. Take this as an olive branch. Otherwise, I'll pursue legal action." My arms were planted by my side.

He didn't waver. "You're assuming Leah wants to leave Brown Brothers. Seems to me she is good right where she is."

My hands started to ball into fists. *He's not worth it.*

"But if she decides to leave, I won't stop her. Anything else, *Mr. Green?* If not, I have a business to run and would appreciate it if you forgot how to navigate to my office in the future."

He snickered. "Next time, I assure you won't make it past reception."

I walked to his door and held it open. "Make sure there isn't a need for a *next time*."

I found Leah at her desk. Her head was down with a sketch in front of her. I tapped the wall of the cubicle to get her attention. When she looked up there was a small smile on her face, but it fell as our eyes connected. "I didn't realize you were here." She looked behind her toward Jacob's office. "Is everything okay?" She stood from her seat.

"Now it is." I felt the adrenaline still pumping through me and wanted to pull her closer. I wanted to kiss her lips, caress her face. I didn't though. I kept my cool and asked, "Can I speak to you for a minute?" I looked at the cubicles surrounding us and said, "Outside?"

She looked down at her laptop and closed it before she answered, "Yes."

I led us to the elevator and watched the doors open. I stepped on behind her, squeezing inside the full car. The two of us remained silent for the ride down. I couldn't guarantee that I wouldn't have wanted to kiss her in the corner if it was only the two of us. *That's if she still would allow it.*

In the fresh air, I took a long inhale. The conversation I had with Jacob tested all my resolve. But I needed to muster a little more to apologize to Leah. I hoped my words wouldn't fall void on her.

"Leah," I took another deep breath, "I was in Jacob's office because I confirmed who leaked the files."

Her mouth dropped open. "I couldn't figure it out." Her words were rushing from her mouth. "I was trying to piece it together but none of it made sense. I wanted this so bad to be over."

I paused. "You were trying to figure it out?"

"Yes. I wanted to get to the bottom of it. I felt bad for not speaking up sooner. It was my notes they were using after all."

"It was a devious plot. One I would have never imagined Jacob would have the audacity to attempt. Especially not with Coco."

Leah stepped back and narrowed her eyes. "Your assistant?"

"My assistant."

"Wow." Her shock mirrored mine when I first found out.

I wiped the back of my neck and hoped the pounding in my head would end. "It's all handled," I told her, "But now I need to apologize to you. For you being in the middle of their scheme. For allowing it to get between us." My eyes fell to the ground. "Leah, I should have trusted you."

Her hand rested on my arm. "We haven't known each other long enough for you to take my word over your friend of many years."

I smirked. "Some friend." I rested my hand over hers. The contact was comforting. "You have never given me a reason to not trust you. And I apologize for thinking you were hiding something from me when it wasn't your business to disclose it."

She mouthed, "Thank you."

"Also," I hesitated. The offer would mean she could be in my space on an everyday basis. I didn't know how I'd be able to ignore my feelings for her, but I'd do what it would take to ensure she was in the best situation. "With everything that has happened, any contracts and non-competes can be voided. And I'd love for you to return to Bryer."

Her face was a beacon of light. Her eyes soft and gentle. The way her lips moved was subtle, but powerful. "You know." I watched each syllable form on her lips. "There are other agencies in Greensboro that I may need to contact. I'm not sure if returning to Bryer is the answer." She looked up to the building. "I am certain I want no parts of how Brown Brothers conducts business either. I need time to transition though."

"Understood." Then I said, "I need to pray a little harder that you'll consider Bryer."

She laughed. "Prayer works, it seems." Her hand fell from my arm. "I should get back inside. I still need this check until I find something else."

We exchanged a knowing look. Mine whispered, "I'd handle everything for you if you let me."

Hers replied, "I don't want you to."

Her back was to mine when I said, "Hey Leah..." When her head turned my way, I said, "Can we start over? Again?"

Her shoulders vibrated from her laugh. "I may have to pray about that." She winked before disappearing into the building.

TWENTY-NINE

Leah

As I waited for the choir to start singing, I prayed, *"God, through it all, please give me peace."* I needed that pressed down, shaken together, and running over. If I was going to make it through another period of applying for jobs and facing potential rejection. Whatever I did I needed to get away from Jacob. I needed a new place to work, and the more I considered it, the less I felt Bryer would be that place. Working for Deshaun didn't seem plausible.

The chords on the piano began, and the choir stood. The first few lyrics of "Something About the Name Jesus" sounded like a soft whisper. As soon as the full choir started singing, I was on my feet. My hands went into the air, and tears streamed down my face. I was singing along with the choir, swaying from side to side, when I felt a hand on my shoulder.

At the end of the song, I turned to the woman beside me

and embraced her. Tears streaming steady down my face. She handed me a tissue, and whispered, "Everything is going to be alright."

I trusted it would be, and in that moment, I felt it would too.

"Thank you," I whispered as the pastor was standing behind the podium.

"It is the sweetest name, I know..." He walked from side to side. "I know many names. I'd like to think my wife's is sweet, that of my baby girl is sweet. Oh," he raised his hand in the air, "but Jesus's name is sweeter." He wiped his hand across his face.

"How many know David?" He took his place behind the podium. "How can we forget him?" He laughed. "David's journey was tumultuous. He had great victories, but also great defeat. He slayed Goliath. But he ran from Saul."

I read along with him as he opened his Bible. Each verse stood out in a different way. By the time he got to Psalm 34, I was encouraged.

"I will praise the Lord at all times," he said with emphasis. "Not when I become king. Or when I slay the giant. Not when I succeed Saul. But at all times." Pastor closed his Bible, wiped his mouth, and asked, "In the midst of your despair, will you still praise Him? When you are going through your valley, will you still praise Him? If things don't go the way you want, will you still praise Him?"

I bowed my head. *"Yes, Lord, I will."*

"Now the doors of the church are open. If you are seeking a closer relationship with God, I invite you to come." At first there was no one, then a slow clap started. I looked to my left as a familiar face made his way down the aisle. His eyes were glistening as they focused on each step ahead of him. I stood clapping as he stood in front of the altar.

Members surrounded him, and a few other people joined him from the audience. As he stood there, David's battles, his victories, and his praise reminded me of Deshaun. In the last week alone, he won a new client, then faced betrayal twice.

My heart sunk thinking about Janine, and if she could ever do what Jacob did. I couldn't imagine it. *"Dear God, please bless Deshaun. Allow him to have a forgiving heart. Allow him to find peace as he moves past these situations. Amen."*

After the benediction, I greeted the women around me. Hugging each and feeling much lighter as I did. A group of people surrounded Deshaun. Some men shaking his hand, women smiling wide in his face. I stood by and waited for them to leave his side. When his eyes found mine though, he maneuvered through the crowd of people and approached me.

"Congratulations on taking that walk." I stretched my arms wide to embrace him. "I'm thankful to have seen it," I whispered in his ear.

"It felt..." he pulled away "necessary."

"And now how do you feel?"

With a wide smile and gentle eyes, he said, "Blessed." The church was clearing out around us. He placed his hand on an empty pew before he asked, "Can I take you to brunch?"

I looked down at my hands then back to him and said, "You know, I'd like that." I smiled as he led me outside. We agreed to leave my car at the church so that he could drive.

I couldn't decide on a restaurant, and Deshaun teased, "We could always fire up the plane and pick a country to visit."

I laughed. "Like it'd be any easier for me to find us a place to eat in a different country." Then I snickered. "Besides, I'm a little hungry." As he continued driving, I said, "There's a spot by campus. The Cracked Egg. That'll work."

"The Cracked Egg it is." He turned at the light to head in the direction of campus.

"How have things been for you at work this week?"

Losing Coco had to be challenging. I didn't know what she did on the daily, but if she was a decent assistant he'd miss her presence.

Deshaun explained, "Every day is a reminder of how two people I trusted betrayed me. I can find someone to replace Coco, but it'll take time before I can forgive her or Jacob for what they did. Not sure our friendship will ever be the same."

"Deshaun," I sighed, "I'm sorry all this happened to you."

He tilted his head to the side. "It was a reality check." His voice was faint as he continued, "You taught me more than I was willing to appreciate at the time."

His face eased but his gaze was on the traffic ahead of us. I didn't interrupt where his mind had wandered, although I wanted to know more. I wanted to dig deeper.

He pulled the car into a parking spot, and The Cracked Egg sat beside us. It looked packed from the window, but when we walked in they sat us right away. I focused on the menu, and he did the same.

"When I left Jacob's office the other day." Deshaun rested his menu to the side of him. "He said something that stung more than what he did to me." His finger traced the fork in front of him. "He said it was *just business. Nothing personal.*"

I cringed. For someone who was all about business, I didn't doubt the words still hit him hard.

"Yeah." He adjusted in his seat. "That full circle moment

made me realize something. I shouldn't approach life, business or personal, like that anymore. I can do better. Relationships, whether professional or not, are important and should have the utmost respect. *Kindness*." His eyes stilled on me.

Everything around us stopped. The crying baby, the shuffling kids, the servers delivering food. It all paused. The only thing still moving was my heart. It was beating a thunderous drum in my chest.

"I can be more than a successful businessman. I can be a good person. Your life, your faith, it has been a good example of how I could walk that path."

My entire body vibrated. I wanted to spring from my chair and hop into his lap. I wanted to wrap my arms around him. Stare into his eyes and kiss his lips. I didn't though. I stayed in my seat as my cheeks warmed and tugged into a wide grin. "That's one of the most humbling compliments I've ever received."

"You're one of a kind, Leah."

If I could have stood up to rejoice, hands raised in the air, without everyone staring at me, I would have. "I'm thankful my kindness could rub off on you. I do think the good person you desire to be for everyone around you will be an admirable characteristic. I'm sure those you encounter will appreciate it."

"I hope so." He looked over his shoulder as the server approached. "There is one person in particular I'm intentional about getting to appreciate me."

"Oh yeah?" I narrowed my eyes and leaned in closer. "Who is that?"

The server stood beside us. "How can I help you today?"

We ordered our food and watched her walk away.

"Leah," Deshaun reached across the table for my hand, "this past year has been a whirlwind—"

I smirked. "To say the least." I exhaled.

We sat for a moment before he continued. "Through the good, the bad, the ups, and the downs. The betrayal. The only thing that hadn't flipped upside down, turned inside out, is the way I feel about you. The desire..." He leaned over the table a little further. "To be near you. To learn more about you." He lifted my hand up to his lips, and my whole body felt hot.

"Deshaun." I tried to speak and maintain my composure. To not sound like I was melting from his touch. "I would love everything about that." I shared, "We've had our moments." My nose scrunched. "But somehow, there isn't anyone I'd rather be around than you."

It was a realization that came to me over the holidays. The longer we spent apart, the stronger the feeling grew. He was always on my mind. In the early morning, late at night. In the middle of a long day. Thinking of him would bring a smile to my face.

Deshaun looked up to the ceiling and pointed. "God works fast when you're on His team, huh?"

I laughed. "I guess you can say that." There was something that still had me curious from our time away from each other. "Can I ask you something?"

"Anything."

"Did you make a donation to the community center?"

His smile wavered before he said, "Don't quote because I'm far from a Bible scholar. And you know, I recently gave my life to God." He smiled a little harder. "There is a scripture that says something about giving in *private*. Or not letting the right hand," he lifted my hand, "know what the left hand is doing." He raised his left hand and shrugged. "Something like that, right?"

He was right. "In that case, you should know that someone gave a hefty donation to the community center. And it will impact many lives."

"Good." His finger stroked the back of my hand. "Anyone who needs help should be able to receive it."

He released my hand, and I missed the warmth. I looked down at where my hand sat on the table before placing it in my lap.

"I've been thinking about my parents' business and accepting the position of CEO."

My mouth opened and my eyes widened. That revelation was more profound than him wanting to be kind to the people around him. Although, in a way, I guess it was all related.

"I don't think there will be any harm to my legacy if I ensure theirs is secure."

The server returned with our plates. Before I bowed my head to pray, Deshaun asked, "Can I?"

"Of course."

He prayed, "God, please bless this food we are about to consume. The people who prepared it, and the company seated at the table. Thank you for this opportunity to break bread with one of your angels." He cleared his throat. "Amen."

I had to wait before opening my eyes. The sting of tears was strong. I moved my napkin to the corner of one eye, before dabbing the other. "Deshaun, that was..."

"It was a long time coming."

I cut into my pancake and let the taste of buttery maple syrup rest on my tongue before swallowing. "And what you want to do for your family is amazing. What will you do with Bryer and your other agencies though?"

"Well," he said after resting his fork on the table. "I'll need a knowledgeable CEO for Vision Creative Studios, which includes Bryer. Someone I can trust."

"I hope you'll be able to find someone who can step in and lead your company until you are ready to return."

His response was sudden. "I already have." He watched me as another bite went into my mouth. "Leah, will you take the reign of my agencies?"

"Agencies?" I coughed. "Plural?" I felt my cheeks warm, and not the way they warmed earlier when we were talking. In a way that felt like I was getting sick. Like the food I consumed would come back up my throat. I needed a drink. I reached across the table and guzzled half the glass of water. When I finished, I eyed him. "Deshaun." I shook my head. "I can't do that." Before leaving Bryer, I was on track to become VP of creative. But CEO? As in the head of the entire company, all the companies. "There's no way that's a good idea."

His voice was smooth as he said, "I've put a lot of thought into it. You are one of the best marketers I know. You have what it takes to lead a team of people. People who will be willing to do what it takes to ensure you succeed."

My head was shaking left to right as he spoke.

He continued, his voice still calm, despite my panic. "Wherever you aren't comfortable, I'll be there to assist. I can get you an assistant to help keep track of the remedial things. Someone the both of us can trust." He laughed mockingly. "Think about it."

"Deshaun," I sighed, "I was thinking this was a reconciliation meal for the two of *us*." I looked at my pancakes, a few bites missing. "Not this." Somewhere deep down, below the surface, I felt my heart sink. I wanted us to be on a path working toward a future together. Him putting business first, again, felt like a slight.

"Oh, it's that too." He winked. "But only if you'd be okay with having both a business and a personal relationship with me. Otherwise, I rescind the offer of CEO."

Eyes blinking, I was speechless. I cut more of my pancakes and chewed until there wasn't much to swallow. I looked across the table. Unlike me, Deshaun's face didn't show any signs of despair. It was quite the opposite, he looked peaceful. "You've offered me something I never even imagined for myself," I said. "I would want the personal and can only imagine the business could make that a challenge. At some point, crossing those lines could cause more issues than it'll solve." I closed my eyes and waited as the air I breathed passed through my nose.

He was quiet as I came to a conclusion.

"I'll need to pray about this." I wiped the napkin across my mouth. "Like seriously seek God."

His fork hovered in front of his lips as he said, "I'd expect nothing less."

THIRTY

3 MONTHS LATER...

Deshaun

Our parents would be proud to see their kids around the table. A table they created, crafted, poured into for years. It took some time, but I finally saw the importance of ensuring their legacy remained intact.

"Think we should snap another picture to capture this moment?" Bianca asked, pulling her phone up and moving to stand between me and Davion. We'd been sending our parents pictures since they set sail for their months-long cruise.

"C'mon," I said with a frown. "Then it's back to business." I tried to maintain my role, when we were in the office, but with those two by my side it was hard. I didn't think I'd enjoy working with them as much as I did. But there was something underrated about having family I could trust to support me.

"Yeah, yeah," Davion said, standing beside Bianca. "Take this pic and smile wide, golden child," he teased.

I joined the two of them as Bianca stretched her arms out in front of us. She took three pictures before she liked what she saw. "Okay, this is a good one." She nudged me in the side. "Your smile is so much brighter these days."

Davion sat in his seat and said, "Uh huh, I remember those early days of me and Tiana. I was walking around smiling like that too." He picked up his notepad and twirled a pen between his fingers. "You never did tell us what the deciding factor was for you. Why you decided to step over to the wild side with us." He tilted his head to the side and guessed, "Was it Leah? Did you believe in her that much, or—"

Bianca smacked her lips. "All this time I was thinking it was because you loved us." She crossed her arms over her chest. "That's not it?"

I leaned back in my seat and looked between the two of them. "Growing my business, my focus had always been on me and what I could do. How far I could expand." My jaw flinched. "Not so much on how I could help others."

The pen in Davion's hand paused, and Bianca stared at me with her eyes narrowed.

"Life is much more than what I can do for myself. Mom and Dad needed the opportunity to enjoy life. They've done so much for us. The least I can I do is help them do that." My jaw eased, and my shoulders relaxed.

"Hmm..." Davion exchanged a look with Bianca but didn't argue my point.

Bianca called me out though. "And it had nothing to do with Leah?" Her lips twisted to the side.

The day I met Leah, changed me. Before her, I was nowhere near considering a woman in my life. I was pursuing my business and nothing else. Then, her invite to church, that changed my soul for an eternity. I wasn't in church all Sundays, but I found myself there most Sundays. Not only because she was there, but because I wanted to be there too.

I explained, "She was the catalyst to set the train in motion, but I can't say she is the reason. She was a good example of how I wanted to live my life though."

Bianca clapped her hands then pointed. "See. That right there. I need a man to come along and act like he knows what I can do for his life."

I cocked my head to the side. "I thought you had..." I snapped my fingers together. "What's his name?"

She rolled her eyes and stood from the table. From the door she said, "He didn't realize what he had in front of him. But I'm glad you did. Leah seems to be a cool chick." Her eyebrows danced. "I can't wait for her to be my sister-in-law." She left the room with a fit of laughter trailing behind her.

As me and Davion walked toward the door, I told him, "She ran out before I could tell you what I needed to say."

He looked at me and his head hung. Much like he did when he thought I was giving him a task that he couldn't manage.

I laughed. "I'm not about to give you something you can't handle." Then I measured the weight of my next words. Sticking my hands in the air and shifting them in front of me. "I'm going to make sure the two of you have everything you need to take over." I added, "I don't plan on staying around here forever."

"But what about Leah? You'll push her aside at the agency?" He worried his lip between his teeth.

"No." I shook my head. "She's doing an amazing job. I can focus on some other things."

Davion put a hand on my shoulder. "I'm happy for you, man. Really, I am. Hope you'll stick around for a while. I like having you here."

I rubbed the top of his head. Even though he was nowhere near the height he was when we were kids. Back when I towered over him. Now we were eye to eye. "Thanks, man. I like being here too." Then I laughed. "I'm about to go check on my lady though."

"Tell me what type of tux I need for the big day," he bolstered. "It's clear you are all in. Considering your best friend is out, I'm the next best person to hold that best man spot."

I cringed.

He laughed. "Too soon?"

"Don't know if it will ever not be too soon." I pulled him into a hug. "When the time comes for me to walk down that aisle, I'd like for you to be standing beside me." I patted his back. *"When the time comes."*

The open sign flashed at *Cup of Sunshine* on my way into the Bryer office. Before I walked into the lobby, I ran over to the café. The line was short, and at the counter I recited Leah's order, followed by my own. The girl who was there when I met Leah smiled wide and asked, "On your way to see Leah?"

I handed her my card and said, "I am," with a grin.

"Tell her I miss her around here."

"I'll do that." With the two cups of coffee in my hand, I

walked over to the office. Taking a sip of mine, I sighed. *Just the way I like it.* I didn't expect the flurry of emotions and memories that flooded me next. The day I stumbled over my order in front of Leah, or how Coco would always have a cup of coffee ready for me. My face formed a frown as I approached the receptionist.

"Mr. Green, everything okay?"

My eyes snapped her way, and I said, "It is. How's everything with you?"

Her eyes wandered around before she gulped. "Everything is great, Mr. Green. Leah is in her..." Her eyes widened. "Your office."

I laughed. "You were right the first time. It's her office. I'm going to go on in," I said as I walked through the doors leading to the cubicles. The people, the noise, the buzz in the office was different from our family headquarters. I couldn't say I didn't miss the creativity, the thrill of winning new clients.

"Mr. Green," I heard from beside me.

"Margot?" I jerked my head back. "I didn't see you there." She saddled beside me, walking the hallway toward Leah's office. "How are you?" Since Leah became CEO, I didn't interact with the staff as much. I wanted her to know I trusted her direction.

Margot stopped walking and so did I. "I'm doing well." Her eyebrows narrowed, then she said, "But I should say I wasn't sure about Leah becoming the CEO." Margot's arms stretched wide in front of her.

I defended my decision by telling her, "I know Leah wasn't the expected choice. But I trust her to make the right decisions. To enlist the people necessary to lead my agencies where they need to go." At one point, Leah reported to

Margot. But Leah didn't mention the role reversal causing any issues for her.

"As do I." Margot's response was firm, and her smile even wider. "She has far exceeded my expectations with the things she has been able to accomplish." She raised her shoulders. "I won't tell you that things are better around here because the *previous* CEO may take offense to that."

I looked down at both cups of coffee in my hand before taking a sip of mine.

"It's good to see you though, Mr. Green."

"Good seeing you too." I held my cup in the air and continued my path to Leah. I tapped on her door and waited for her voice.

"Come in." She sat behind the desk. Her head was down as it was most of the time when she was reviewing documents, proposals, or creative. She was serious about her role. Although I insisted she delegate most of the work, she remained engaged in the day-to-day activities.

"Hope I'm not disturbing you, Ms. Moore."

Her eyes flicked up before she stood from her seat. With a smirk, she said, "A little." She pinched her fingers in front of her. "But it's a worthy distraction. What do I owe the pleasure?"

I placed my cup of coffee on her desk, and she grabbed the one I had outstretched to her. "I was in a meeting with my team and was reminded of this amazing woman I can call my own. I wanted to see her. Make sure it wasn't all some crazy dream." I moved behind the desk and took her in my arms.

She sipped from the coffee before putting it down. "To think when we met you didn't even remember your own order."

I scoffed. "Amazing how much can change in a year."

"Can't believe this is my reality." She placed the cup down and turned toward me. "That I'm here in this office where I was praying for a promotion on one team. God showed up, and showed all the way out, giving me *teams*." She relaxed further into my arms, wrapping hers around my waist. "And you." She pecked my lips. "I'd say you are the icing on the cake, but that wouldn't even scratch the surface of what you mean to me."

"Speaking of which..." I stared into her eyes. "I have something else I wanted to tell you." Her muscles tensed under my grip. "I thought of all the ways I wanted to say this, but nothing felt more appropriate."

She eased away from me. Took a small step back. "Deshaun?"

I stepped toward her and pulled her back into my arms. I stroked my thumb under her lips before kissing them again. When I pulled away, I whispered, "Leah, you have made me immeasurably happy. I love you."

She gasped and flung her hand over her mouth. Through her clenched fingers, she said, "Deshaun, I don't know what to say. You've done nothing but show me how much you care. And I hope I've reciprocated in the way you need. The way you want."

"You don't have to say anything. Not now. Not until you're ready." I could have spent the entire day looking at her. There was something magnetic about her that drew me in. *Thank you, God, for this woman.*

"Except." She grasped my hands in hers. "I didn't expect any of this. I didn't expect you to be the man I prayed for before I even knew you existed. Or for you to leap over my expectations of what I thought God could bless me with." Her head hung and she laughed. "Especially not with our rocky start."

"Rocky?"

She cocked her brow.

I admitted, "Okay, it was a little rocky."

"But now, I couldn't imagine life without you." Her hand caressed my cheek. "Deshaun, I love you."

EPILOGUE
2 YEARS LATER...

Leah

"I'm so glad to see you two still together," Ms. Carol beamed as Deshaun and I walked into the kitchen of the community center. Since the *anonymous* donation, a lot had changed there.

The building had expanded, the kitchen renovated and much larger than it was before. The living quarters doubled in size and kept Liam busy. But he was happy he didn't have to turn away as many people each night.

Of everything that happened over the years, the community center improvements were the greatest.

Well, kinda.

"We are glad to be here." I looked at Deshaun and the smile I wore, mirrored on his face.

Deshaun was the greatest thing that happened to me. He was the greatest surprise, and each day he kept surprising me.

His kindness, when unlocked, was unmatched. He went above and beyond for most of the people in his life. Even for strangers he didn't know. It was like he needed to trust that his kindness wasn't a weakness. Once he realized that, he wore it like a badge of honor.

I couldn't be prouder to stand beside him. Especially as we volunteered at the community center. Even though we were each busy with the businesses, we promised we'd take time each week to volunteer.

"I'm waiting on my invitation to the wedding," Ms. Carol sang as her eyes danced between the two of us.

"Ms. Carol." I waved my hand at her. "When it happens, you'll be there." I winked.

I didn't doubt that one day we'd get married, have beautiful babies, and live happily ever after. But if I was being honest, I felt like we were living our happily ever after already. Although we talked about that next step, I wasn't anticipating it. I knew it'd come when the time was right, like everything else God had in store for me.

Deshaun cleared his throat. The apron tangled around his neck, as his hands fussed with it. "Ms. Carol," he said, looking up from the knot, "where'd you like me today?"

"Today, I want you baking that chicken again. Like last week." She put her hand on her hip. "Someone had the nerve to tell me it was better than mine."

Deshaun shook his head. "Imagine that."

"It's okay, baby. I take credit for teaching you a thing or two in this kitchen. You bypassed what I taught you, and that's okay."

I laughed at the two of them before I walked out to the dining area to ensure the tables and chairs were set.

"Sis," I heard Liam's voice ring out. "What are you doing here?"

I tilted my head, but before I could remind him we were in there the same day every week, he shook his head.

"Never mind," he countered. "I need to go check some paperwork." He started moving toward the door, away from me. "I'll see you later."

I continued through the dining room, wiping tables and moving chairs. An hour later, the volunteers were bringing out food. The members lined up and were ready to eat.

After we served the last person, I looked at Deshaun and told him, "Ms. Carol was right. That chicken looked amazing." I rubbed my stomach. "Too bad there isn't any more left."

He pulled me into him, our aprons swiping against each other. I felt his soft lips on my forehead before he said, "Is my baby hungry?"

I snuggled into his neck and said, "I am."

"Good. Let me take you to get something to eat."

I snatched my apron from around my neck and wrinkled it in my hands. "As long as it's not like our first date when you kidnapped me. Had me starving for hours." I tossed my apron in the trash and headed for the door.

But his soft laugh under his breath made my feet stop moving.

"Deshaun?" I watched as his eyes wandered the center. "You aren't?"

"There's one thing I promise," he held the door open, "to always keep things interesting."

Grumbling stomach. Hunger pains. Nothing stopped me from being giddy as we drove outside of the Greensboro city limits toward the executive airfield. As we climbed out of the car though, I hoped wherever he was taking me wouldn't take too long.

"There's nothing that'll top the Italian grandmother in that New York kitchen." I was rambling on about the food and wine when I didn't hear his footsteps beside me.

Deshaun wasn't beside me as I walked toward the plane. He was feet behind me rolling two suitcases. "What are those for?" I scanned my memory for the next day's schedule. "I have meetings on the calendar for tomorrow," was all I could say without looking at my phone for the details.

"Baby," he said, cupping my chin, "It's handled. C'mon."

I followed behind him as my stomach twisted and turned. Not because I was hungry but worried about what *it's handled* meant. Was that he canceled my meetings? Or has someone sitting in on them? Would staff be calling me while we were away?

Naila greeted us at the top of the stairs. "Ms. Moore, need anything?"

Deshaun answered for me, telling her, "A glass of wine to settle her nerves, please."

Naila grabbed our luggage and said, "I'll have that for you soon." She disappeared to the back of the plane, and I stood near the cockpit like it was my first time on the jet.

"I hope you two are ready for..." Jeremy stopped with a look to Deshaun. "Wheels up shortly." He disappeared before I could question him.

"What's going on?" I asked Deshaun as we sat across from each other. "My brother was acting weird at the center. Jeremy looks like he was about to reveal a government secret." My eyes narrowed. "Where are we going?"

Deshaun's response wasn't what I hoped for. "Let's check

with Naila to see what snacks she has. Then you can rest until we arrive." The part about a snack sounded great, the rest until we arrived at some unknown location didn't sound as nice.

There was luggage, enough time to rest. "Okay, so not a quick trip to New York." I watched Naila as she approached with a glass of wine for both of us. "Are we flying to the West Coast?"

Deshaun shook his head. "We'll take the tray of snacks, please," he said to Naila before she disappeared again. *A full tray of snacks.*

I regretted not being on a commercial flight. One where the flight attendant would announce our destination. Instead, I engaged Deshaun in a game of twenty questions. A game that I failed. Questions about our destination, he wouldn't budge.

"Before we arrive, we'll shower and get changed for our meal." He relaxed into his seat, and I tried to resemble his posture. But the unknown was taunting me.

"Dinner. You mean dinner, right?" I looked at my watch. It was still evening in North Carolina. I was hoping he'd slip up and give me a clue to where we were going with a reference to the time.

He didn't.

I asked, "If we are leaving the country, did you grab my passport?" In recent months, he ensured that was a priority on my task list. *In case we decided to hop on an international flight.* At the time, I did it to appease him. I knew neither of us had time to leave the country. The agencies were flourishing, and so were the restaurants. It left little time for dates around Greensboro, let alone outside of the country. *If only the clouds could give signs of our destination.*

"Tell me again about the dream house you want to live in."

He settled in his seat like the description would be a late-night tale to put him to sleep.

I thought about my dream house often. Especially after moving from my parents' house. The small condo downtown wasn't someplace I wanted to make a permanent home. I wanted a big house, on sprawling land.

"It'll have enough room for our family," I said with a smile. "An office for you and me." I could imagine the two of us working at home together some days. Although rushing between meetings we could steal a kiss, a quick conversation. "A large kitchen. Like your parents have. For us to cook a Sunday dinner and have both families there."

"Ehm," he hummed. "Sounds luxurious." He winked. "A little lavish even."

"Someone reminded me that we should live like Heaven on earth. That our God wants us to have an abundant life. And we can do that *while* we help others. Right?" It took me a while to adjust to the amount of money that Deshaun had. But I found that having more allowed me to help more. My donations to the community center were plentiful each year after becoming CEO. The help I was able to give my parents was immeasurable.

"Right. And I can't wait to see this house full of love you describe."

My eyes were starting to get heavy. The *house tale* took a toll on me too. I rested my head against the headrest.

"I'll wake you when it's time for us to change." Deshaun's gaze turned toward the clouds instead of his eyes shutting.

There were soft taps on my knee, then a breath on my neck as I heard, "Leah," whispered in my ear.

"Hey," I whispered. "Are we landing soon?"

He nodded and kissed my cheek. Before he moved I stretched my arms out and rested them on his neck. Gazing into his eyes, I prayed, *"Thank you God for allowing this man to come into my life. For everything you've blessed me with. And the lessons you taught me along the way."*

"What'd you packed for me?" I rose from my seat as Deshaun settled back into his. I unzipped the hanging luggage behind the door. There were a few outfits, different options, and other casual clothes. "Wait," I peeped my head through the crack, "how long are we staying?"

A devious grin spread across Deshaun's face before he said, "The blue dress will look amazing on you tonight." He walked toward me. "I hope you like it."

I pulled it out and hung it against my body. "Gorgeous."

"And so are you."

I changed into the dress, then sat back in my seat. Deshaun went to the room and emerged with a tailored suit and tie matching my dress. I couldn't hide my excitement. "Not a clue even?" The two of us together could have walked a red carpet or had dinner with the queen. The anticipation was killing me.

"You'll know soon enough."

The plane descended soon after. He held my hand as we stepped out into the hanger. Our passports appeared in his hands as he gave them to the man who greeted us.

"Enjoy your time in Italy, Mr. Green."

Once we were away from the agent, I gushed, "Italy?" I tugged on his hand. "We are in Italy?"

The sun shined bright among a field in front of us. "I hope you don't mind we missed dinner."

My stomach rumbled and I laughed. "For this trip, my stomach can manage."

We rode in the car admiring the landscape. It was breath-taking, and worth every minute of anticipation. When the car stopped, I was awestruck. The cliffside château, overlooking the electric blue lake was breathtaking. "Wow, look at God's beauty."

He kissed behind my ear. "Isn't she beautiful?"

My cheeks were already burning from the sheer beauty of the countryside. Experiencing it with Deshaun made it that much more glorious. But as we approached the entrance of the restaurant my eyes narrowed. "There isn't anyone here." Not a single person sat inside.

He turned toward me and said, "It's only us." He eyed me. "I hope this isn't too much."

Tears prickled the back of my eyes. I reached my hand to the side of his face and said, "No, it's not."

"Welcome." A beautiful, dark-haired woman stood behind him. She uttered a line in Italian, then said, "Right this way."

Our table had a view of the lake, and I couldn't stop staring at it. The still waters had a calming effect. The sun's rays as it beamed down on it lifted my spirits in ways I couldn't have imagined. "Do you see that?" I turned toward Deshaun, but he wasn't seated across from me anymore.

"I was trying to wait." He kneeled on the ground beside me. "I can't anymore. I don't want another minute to pass by."

My mouth fell open. The tears that were threatening to fall earlier were streaming down my face.

He flicked a few of them, but the rest were relentless. "Over these last couple of years, you have become the most important person in my life. The person I can't wait to greet early in the morning, and I go to sleep thinking of at night. My life now has purpose beyond me. And..." He reached into his pocket and pulled out a box. "I want to spend every day that God blesses me with, with you. Will you marry me?"

I closed my eyes as the tears became uncontrollable. Through closed eyes and shaky hands beside me, I said, "There isn't anything more I want." I reached for his face and pulled it toward mine.

He stood from the floor and wrapped his arms around me. Although the tears were falling, everything within me was still.

The End

PRAISE

If you enjoyed this story, I'd love for you to leave a review on your favorite retailer, or Goodreads, and if you are feeling generous share it with your friend group.

I appreciate the love and support!

ALSO BY FAITH ARCENEAUX

If you enjoyed Love is Patient, and are looking for your next read, consider continuing the series:

- Love is Hopeful

For a full list of books, visit: https://bit.ly/faith2loveBooks

ABOUT THE AUTHOR

Faith Arceneaux is a Christian Romance author who believes
1 Corinthians 13, "Three things will last forever — faith, hope,
and love — and the greatest of these is love." Through her
storytelling, Faith prays that readers will not only be enter-
tained, but will have a renewed faith to love.

Printed in Great Britain
by Amazon

42858625R00139